by Tom Clark

Airplanes (1966)
The Sandburg (1966)
Emperor of the Animals (1967)
Bun (1968)
Stones (1969)
Air (1970)
Car Wash (1970)
Neil Young (1971)
The No Book (1971)
Green (1971)
Smack (1972)
John's Heart (1972)
Back in Boston (1972)
Blue (1974)
Chicago (1974)
Suite (1974)
At Malibu (1975)
Fan Poems (1976)
Baseball (1976)
Champagne and Baloney (1976)
35 (1976)
No Big Deal (1977)
How I Broke In (1977)
The Mutabilitie of the Englishe Lyrick (1978)
When Things Get Tough on Easy Street: Selected Poems
     1963-1978 (1978)
The World of Damon Runyon (1978)
One Last Round for The Shuffler (1979)
The Master (1979)
Who Is Sylvia? (1979)
The Great Naropa Poetry Wars (1980)
The Last Gas Station and Other Stories (1980)

TOM
THE
GAS
AND

CLARK

LAST STATION OTHER STORIES.

Black Sparrow Press — Santa Barbara — 1980

8/1980
Am Lit. Coll

THE LAST GAS STATION AND OTHER STORIES.
Copyright © 1980 by Tom Clark.

ACKNOWLEDGEMENT

Some of these stories first appeared in *Boulder Monthly*, *On the Mesa*, *Sparrow*, *The World*, *Stones*, *John's Heart*, and *The Rolling Stone*.

LIBRARY OF CONGRESS CATALOGING IN PUBLICATION DATA

Clark, Tom, 1941-
    The last gas station and other stories.

    I. Title.
PZ4.C5955Las   813'.54   80-36765
ISBN 0-87685-457-9
ISBN 0-87685-458-7 (signed ed.)
ISBN 0-87685-456-0 (pbk.)

to Angelica

TABLE OF CONTENTS

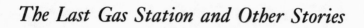

The Last Gas Station and Other Stories

Famous Last Words

1.

She smiled hello at him every day for one year on that downtown corner, then one day she said:

"What do you do?"

"Oh, I don't know. Write I guess. Poems, stories, something like that. I'm unemployed at present."

"You mean you're *free lance?*"

"Call me independent."

She gave him the eye, head to toe, then smiled again.

"Oh, you just—loaf?"

"You can call it that, I guess."

"But don't you ever feel like *doing* anything—like other people do?"

"Why should I?"

"If you're going to get upset, maybe we'd better stop talking about it."

When she smiled a third time, her belly wriggled in the ancient way under the blue print dress on which floated what looked to him like grapefruit or oranges.

The sun beat down on the metropolitan Los Angeles intersection; his eyes hooked with hers for a swimming instant then suddenly the light changed, the traffic poured over their bodies like crushed ice, nobody said anything. They crossed the street.

They didn't know where they were going.

2. Her Place

"Well—is there something *on* me?"

"No . . . Why?"

"You've been looking at me—for an hour!"

"I was looking at your dress."

"Is there anything—the *matter* with it?"

"It's just—"

"What's *wrong* with my dress?"

"Why—nothing particular."

"Please, I want to know." She leaned forward suddenly and breathed flames on him. He flinched.

"Why, I find you exciting, that's all."

"Is it something I'm doing?"

"I didn't notice you doing anything."

"Is it my legs—is that it?"

"What?"

"Stop staring at my legs!"

"I'm trying."

She reached for her drink, changed her mind, grabbed a cigarette instead, and simply by holding it up to her mouth lit it.

He mumbled her name.

3. Fumbling

She pulled her dress up.

"What do you want?" she asked him.

"To look the Old Man in the eye, that's all."

"What old man?"

"You know what I mean."

"Have you got cold feet, or what?"

"No, just feeling the strain." He was sweating.

Her smile came out of a body that was tawny yet slick like a shark's.

"Shut up," she said.

"I don't want to."

"I don't *want* you to, for Christ's sake."

"I don't generally change my mind, once it's made up, you know." Now she was smiling, because he was ridiculous, having said that.

"You can if you want to," she said.

"Shut up," he explained.

"I don't want you to."

"Neither do I."

And that was the last word either of them said.

12

A Late Valentine

A pretty girl with clear honorable eyes—a cowgirl. She wore denims and buckskins and lived in her parents' ranch-style home. There was nothing premeditated about her. She had no mental side. She simply made men conscious to the highest degree of her physical loveliness. He had no desire to change her. Her deficiencies were knit up with a passionate energy that transcended and justified them. He would crawl across America to win her. He intended to arrive on Valentine's Day.

Even at the beginning the gusts were blowing with a sound like rhinoceroses make when they charge through wind tunnels. It was late in October, but in those hills winter had already started. He strapped to his knees a pair of bulky, well-worn goalie pads with ten layers of padding underneath—a gift of the local hockey team—and set out. Grit and dust blew in his face, the rhino wind buffeted him. The road was covered with ice, with snow; it was real hard going. As he crawled he gripped a bar with two tricycle wheels on each end. The tricycle wheels spun on the snow and ice. It bothered him a little but he gritted his teeth for love and kept going.

Unfriendly animals trailed him all across Missouri: dogs, cats, ants, skunks, cougars, myna birds. He couldn't shake them off, not for love or money. He threw them dollar bills, hot dogs, dimestore jewelry, but still they clung to his heels. He was nearly insane by the time he reached the state line. He crossed it and looked back. All he could see was a thin blue line of mountains in the distance, into which the sun was setting like a gigantic bruise from which dark arteries spread themselves over a poisoned sky. It was twelve degrees below zero and he had fifteen hundred miles to crawl before he could stand up on his feet again.

In Pennsylvania he paused for a week for the sake of love to found a city of crawlers. Inspired by his example, men took ridiculous causes seriously, and debased themselves on behalf of their ideals. Degraded, humiliated, they formed ranks behind his two-

13

wheeled crawler and followed him up and down the road all day, until it got dark. After the seventh day he got out of town by cover of night.

As he was crawling over the Blue Ridge Mountains, a couple of good old boys in a pickup truck stopped to talk to him. "They were running me through the mill," he said. "One of them asked me where I got the money to do this and I looked down in the grass and saw a crumpled-up dollar bill. I told them, 'Every now and then I just reach down and pick up a dollar. Love takes care of me.'"

"Buddy, you ought to get a horse," they said. "You're outa your dang mind."

His greatest fear was that he would crawl across America, and she wouldn't be home when he got there.

"I guess it cost me between $8,000 and $10,000," he told us later, "counting the time I lost on the job, and all the hamburgers I ate along the way. It would have been worth it if. . . ." His voice trailed off. Love had left him verbally destitute.

He reached her house at five o'clock in the morning on March the 10th. He crawled up her front steps and pounded on her front door. She came out after a while and told him to be quiet, he was going to wake up her folks. She wouldn't let him in. "But I love you," he said. Excitement made him speak much too loud.

She went inside and called the police. Outside it was just beginning to get light. As they took him away he could see her there, standing behind the plexiglass window, her clear honorable eyes telling him she wasn't home. It was at that point he got religion.

Lover Boy

Hitchhiking you meet all kinds.

The other day a guy in a white VW bus picks me up at the Lake Eldora ski turnoff.

"Where you going?"

"Idaho Springs."

"I'll take you."

"But it's forty-five miles."

"Shit, that ain't nothin'."

He tells me his life story. "I'm retired. I'm fifty-seven years old. Got a wife and four kids in Kansas City. Bought this bus last year, never had so much fun in my life as I've had since then. Drive around to all the ski areas and wait at the bottom for the honeys to come along. I help 'em put on their chains. One thing leads to another, you know?" He leans across the wheel and winks at me lasciviously. No, I don't know.

We're driving along. There's a girl walking on the other side of the road. Guy slams on his brakes, pulls over, rolls down his window and offers the girl a ride—even though she's going in the opposite direction, north.

"Wanna ride, chickee?"

Girls stares at him, incredulous.

"Come on, honey, we'll take you where you want to go." He gives her the wink.

She shakes her head emphatically. "No thanks."

"Aw, c'mon." He's stopped now, backing up to keep pace with her.

She walks on, refusing to look at him.

He shrugs and gives up, shifts gears, off we go.

"Guess she didn't want to take on both of us," he says matter-of-factly. "Them chicks only got one thing on their minds."

Two weeks later I'm hitching to Eldora when two girls pull over to ask me where they can park. The road up to Lake Eldora's too icy for them. They want to find a place to park. They roll the window down and the sweet smell of perfume flows out into the chilly air. Ever noticed how much better cosmetics smell in the cold?

"Should we park here, is that safe, or should we go back to town, do you think?"

"Got any chains?"

"Yes, but we don't know how to put them on."

"With chains you could make it up that road."

Pause. The pretty one in the blue sweater smiles. "Do *you* know how to put chains on?"

I shake my head no. I'm going somewhere. As I shake my head, out of my eye I see a white VW bus pulling up behind me. It's the guy from Kansas City. He's out of the bus and walking up to us with a big grin on his face before you can say "Jack Robinson."

Just as he's leaning forward to offer his assistance to the two young ladies, they exchange quick, anxious glances, and the girl in the passenger seat rolls up her window. The girl driving gives it the gun in reverse. The next thing we see is their exhaust as they head back to Nederland.

Guy turns to me, squinting through his rimless glasses. He looks every day of his fifty-seven years. He spreads his palms out in a "what can I do?" gesture and grins at me.

"Weren't my type anyhow," he says. The sadness of a lifetime is in his voice as he says this. I get the feeling he is talking less to me than to himself, so I look away.

He plods back to his bus, climbs back up behind the wheel and drives off. His Missouri license plate is the last I see of him. It bears the following letters:

LVR BOY 78

Dissatisfaction

It was the same look she'd had on her face the night he first met her. It made a shiver run from blade to blade of his broad shoulders. He shot her a worried glance.

"What do you mean it did nothing to you?"

"What I say. Nothing, Buck."

"Well, what the hell. I done the same thing with a dozen other girls and they liked it plenty."

"How do you know that, Buck?"

"They told me, that's how."

"Well, I ain't no dozen other girls, Buck. I'm just me, and it didn't do nothing to me. Nothing at all."

"Just what do you expect, for instance?"

"If you don't know, Buck, I can't tell you."

She laughed the hot searing laugh that always left scars on his hearing. He frowned and looked away. She grabbed him and pulled him to her, laughing.

"Buck, I'm the kind of girl that believes in giving a man a second chance."

"I'm sure glad to hear that, honey, because I'm the kind of man that believes if at first you don't succeed, try again."

She smothered him with the pillow. He was half passed-out anyway from all the liquor. She dressed, took his wallet and tiptoed out of the room. She needn't have bothered to tiptoe. He never got a chance to delight another girl.

She took the next plane back to Washington, sitting primly on the plane in her Parisian business suit with her ankles crossed under the seat ahead of her, sipping coffee and reading a financial magazine. Under her reading glasses she wore a look of quiet dissatisfaction.

The Hope Diamond

"It's now if we're going to."

"I'll take your spike."

Smiling, he handed her the hypodermic needle and she plunged it into her arm, which was tied off with the cloth belt of her dress.

She sighed and lay back on the ragged mattress next to him. A deep feeling of peace spread over her which made the bare dusty light bulb over their heads take on the brilliance of the Hope Diamond. It was as happy as she had ever felt since the day they moved into the White House.

Love Story with Hope

Hope came to Boulder from California.

"It's really a neat town," a guy she'd once known in Santa Barbara had said. "Real clean and lots of super people. You'd like it."

Hope forgot about it. A year later she was on her way to New York. Hope made clothes for a living. She was going to New York with a designer friend. They had a new line of clothing to display to a woman they knew who had a fashionable shop on the East Side. The woman had bought their work in the past and Hope had high hopes that this trip would produce another good commercial score.

Hope's designer friend, Howard, was gay. Hope had known him for years. They had driven cross country twice before, from California to New York. On these trips they always slept in the same motel room, keeping each other awake late with long soul-to-soul descriptions of their respective romantic lives. Neither had been very lucky in that regard. Howard never had enough lovers. Hope always had several too many. When they compared notes, Hope learned that Howard was lonely and Howard learned that Hope had different problems. She was what used to be known as the kind of girl who can't say no.

Hope was sexually prodigious, and her problem, if it was a problem, was that she enjoyed sex too much—with practically anybody. Her life was consequently a revolving door proposition; men came and went at a fantastic rate. For a while, Hope entertained the idea of doing what she liked best for money, but when she got around to trying it she found she didn't care much for it. The profit motive, she discovered, crowded all others out. How could you enjoy a man while you were taking money?

One night on their way to New York, Hope and Howard talked about her feelings on this point. Hope couldn't make Howard understand. He proposed a comparison.

"I don't see why you can't have just as much fun when you know your bills are getting paid," he said. "Isn't marriage the same thing?"

"The same thing?" Hope, a slim blonde, tossed her hair as she talked. It was a habit she'd developed as a girl: boys had found it attractive.

"The same thing as going with tricks, I mean." Howard peered in Hope's eyes. He was interested in her, simply as a friend.

Hope's voice was too sharp. "I *hate* going with tricks," she said.

They were sitting on twin beds in a motel room in Laramie, Wyoming, smoking cigarettes in the middle of the night. Outside in the feathery darkness of the motel parking lot snow was falling. New York was 2000 miles away. It was late November.

Howard kept staring at her; it was making Hope nervous. He took a deep drag and stubbed his cigarette out in an ashtray on the table between their beds. "Why?" he said.

"Every time is a super drag," Hope said.

"But aren't some of the men nice?"

Hope tossed her hair.

"Oh, sometimes. Once in a *great* while." Hope was lying on her side, her head propped up with one hand.

"And then?"

"Then nothing." Hope blew a smoke ring at the acoustic paneling on the ceiling.

"And when they're *not* nice?"

"I just completely turn myself off emotionally. And hope they get through real fast."

"Hmm," said Howard. "That sounds awful."

"It is," said Hope. "That's why I don't do it any more." She put out her cigarette, switched off the light and rolled over.

Hope had no particular interest in marrying but she did hope one day to achieve a "lasting relationship," by which she meant one that lasted more than a few weeks. Two months was Hope's all time record.

They drove east through snow to Cheyenne, then south to Boulder where Howard had a friend in the real estate business. The roads were icy and Howard wanted to stop until the weather cleared up. Hope was in no particular hurry; they weren't due in New York for another week. Howard's friend had a big apartment

20

and there was room for him and Hope to stay for a few days.

Their second night in town, Howard's friend invited them to accompany him to a party. At the party Hope met a very attractive man. His name was David. He was also in real estate. He asked Hope to come home with him.

Hope was interested. She hadn't been to bed with anybody for six days. Abstinence always made her tense. She felt like some violin string, tuned to the point where it breaks.

"Sure," she told David. "I'd love to go home with you. After I have another drink."

She had another drink. It relaxed her. She told Howard she was leaving. Howard looked at her hard. David had his arm around her.

"It's all right," Hope told Howard. "I've met this very nice man. I'll see you in the morning."

They went back to David's place and Hope did her thing. She enjoyed herself and was feeling fine afterwards until David started talking business. He asked her what she did for a living.

"I make clothes," Hope said absently.

David ran two fingers along the top of Hope's thigh.

"Ever thought of modeling?"

Hope noticed something in David's tone. Something hard. Whatever it was, she didn't like it.

"Modeling? What kind?" She pushed David's hand away from her leg. He was making her nervous.

"Oh, for individual clients of mine." David's voice was falsely casual. He was watching her now.

"Clients?"

"I meet a lot of people in my business who want to meet girls."

"In the *real estate* business?"

David chuckled. "Shelter isn't everything, you know."

"I'm not sure I follow you," Hope said.

"Yes you do," David said.

"I mean I'm not sure I *want* to follow you."

David smiled. "Well, think it over."

"I'm leaving in a few days anyway," Hope said. "You're going to find somebody else to be your model." She sat up in David's bed and lit a cigarette. He tried to pull her back down, and she wrenched away, jumping out of bed.

Howard was drinking a cup of coffee in his friend's apartment when Hope walked in. She looked upset.

"That was quick," Howard said lightly. "Nice guy?"

Hope shook her head. "A real creep."

Howard sighed. "Ah."

"Let's leave in the morning," Hope said.

"Sure," Howard said. "I've seen enough of this place anyway."

In the morning they were packing their bags when the phone rang. Howard answered it. When he heard who it was, his face fell.

"For you," he told Hope, holding out the receiver. "It's *David.*" Howard's whisper was more like a hiss.

Hope took the phone.

"Hello?"

"It's me." David's voice was as smooth and assured as ever. "Why'd you leave in such a hurry?"

"Why do you think?" Hope's voice was cold.

"You aren't mad about the modeling thing?"

"Why should I be?"

"You *shouldn't.* It was meant as a compliment, you know."

"That's swell." Hope tossed her hair, staring into the receiver. "Did you have anything else to tell me, or is it just *that* business again?"

"I just wanted to tell you how much I liked last night. And to ask you out for dinner tonight."

"Sorry," said Hope. "I'm leaving town."

"A shame," David said, sounding disappointed. "If you'd stay around for a while, we could have a lot of fun."

"You can have fun with somebody else," Hope said, hanging up.

She went on packing her bags. Three days later she and Howard were in New York. Their new line of clothes was a smashing success. In three weeks they made four thousand dollars. Howard sold his car and they flew back to the Coast first class. They were in San Francisco in time for New Year's. Howard threw a party to celebrate the holiday and their good fortune. Hope came in one of her own creations. Several people at the party told her how beautiful she was looking, but Hope tossed her head and passed off the compliments with a graceful lightness. Flattery meant nothing to her. She knew who her friends were. She also knew she wasn't beautiful, even if her clothes were. The fact didn't bother her.

She met a man she liked at the party and took him home with her. Howard spent the night at the party, dancing and drinking. In the morning he slept alone.

One night shortly after New Year's, Howard and Hope were sitting around in Hope's apartment, talking.

Howard looked into Hope's eyes and bells rang.

It was the telephone. Hope answered it. It was David, calling from Boulder.

"I'm busy," Hope said, getting ready to hang up.

"Wait a minute," David said. "I've got to tell you something."

Hope was silent. She glanced at Howard, forming David's name with her mouth. Howard made a face.

"I've got an offer to make," David said.

"Not *that* again."

"Look," David sounded earnest. "This is perfectly straight, Hope. I've got a shot at some business frontage on the Mall. It's a property I can get for half what it's worth. I want to put you in it. Making clothes and selling them."

"I don't believe it."

"I'm totally serious," David said. "This is strictly a business proposition, Hope. I like your work. This town will fall over dead for the kind of stuff you make."

"Since when did you see my work?"

"You showed me pictures, don't you remember?"

"I'll have to think it over," Hope said after a long pause. "I'm busy right now." She hung up and turned to Howard to talk things over.

Hope was in the clothing business in Boulder for two years. She and David were partners; their shop was a raging success. At Hope's request, Howard came to town and went to work for them.

23

Today the three are co-owners of a large women's apparel store in a major city on the East Coast. David is married and has two young sons. He lives on the Coast. Hope and Howard are still single. They share an apartment in Boulder when they are not in the East. They stay up late at night and have a lot of long talks. One night when I was at their house Hope told me this story. You don't hear a story with a happy ending all that often. I pointed that out to Hope.

"You think this is a happy ending?" She tossed her hair and grinned at me, then at Howard.

"She still has her men," Howard said. "We have an understanding with David. Hope has her men, David has the business." Howard paused and laughed, glancing at his blonde comrade, who smiled back at him warmly. "And I have Hope."

The Book of Love

for Joanne Kyger

There is a new arrogance in the dip of her back and the proud curves of her projective buttocks.

Her hand fingers her detached eye with gentle precision as she blackens the lids.

Her over-all air of determined orientalism shows tigerish love while her smart sophistication reveals the supreme importance attached in her lovemaking to neatness of toilet.

*

He approaches her chamber.
Bearing a fly-whisk and a box of betel nuts, he leads her to the bed.

*

She is parted from her lover and driven to distraction by the enchantments of the spring.

Alone with her desires, she strolls in a posh garden, holding in her hand a wand of candy flowers.

There is now a greater refinement in her body, a more conscious delight in feminine charm and gorgeous richness of philosophy.

*

Itching with love, she reclines on the terrace in the sultry stillness of a summer night.

Her drooping pose illustrates a state of longing, for which the only cure will be her lover's return.

Out of the dark trees jaguars glide to brush past her nude skin, which emits a glow like the sky's.

*

She is playing with him as with a yo-yo—the boy, suspended from her finger, jerks nervously up and down in unison with her thoughts.

The ardent character of her brooding is suggested by the brilliant red of her dress.

*

An air of gentle tenderness marks their dalliance.

Her hand shyly strokes his wrist, a reticence implying the exquisite character of her feelings.

She moves on easy lights, lightly easing everyone over to the bed.

*

It is a little after dusk, the full moon just rising over rocky cliffs.

She stands holding a flower while a maid beguiles her with music from inside her vagina. A deer symbolizing the absent lover advances through the trees.

Love and Death

Here's the story: Bob Bunny is alive. I saw him just this morning. He is feeling fine. He says, Tell my mother not to worry. Hope you're reading this, Mrs. Bunny . . . .

Bob Bunny: alive. Bob is a living organism, a mammal. He is part of the animal kingdom. He is a human being. He is a nice guy. He is alive. He has vitality. He is full of spunk. The vital spark of life inhabits him, he lives and breathes, stuff passes through him in an eternal respiration. In the sense that this respiration will continue when Bob is gone, he can be considered immortal, and for Bob's sake it is well to do so. Like everybody else, Bob has his problems. What other people think of him matters. Small remarks linger in his mind for years and blossom into serious hangups.

But Bob is alive. When he eats a peanut butter and jelly sandwich, he does not think of the two bookend-shaped slabs at either end of his sandwich as mere slices of bread; he thinks of them as slices of the *staff of life*. Birds sing, leaves return to the trees in spring, flowers grow, children run and play, ants crawl across the picnic blanket, Bob's wife and kids squabble, but he lolls his head back on the grass and takes in the endless bliss of the sky: immortal. I am part of *that*, Bob thinks.

Bob has a lot to learn. Ahead lies the dark road, tall trees on either side, darkness overhead, the moon dull and stifled, no stars. Suddenly the road emerges out of the clearing and there appears a striking crossroads, lit by the glaring ugly neon of 1962. . . . Bob strides off to mingle his biology with that of Mrs. Bunny, creating additional bunnies.

Bob is animated. His life-blood flows in round veins that are conduits through which gurgle the aerated products of the various parts of his arterial system. There is a bubbling, a foaming; a spuming, spraying, surf of red corpuscles. It is just after lunch. Bob has just eaten a particularly large carrot. He is feeling exceptionally well. He picks up his pen and notebook and begins to record his impressions of a beautiful day: I am alive; I live, breathe, respire and subsist; walk the earth but am nourished by the gods . . . .

Bob struts and frets his hour upon the stage with a smile on his face. Inside he is turbulent; he has depths no one knows. Swirls, eddies. Bob was born. He came into the world. He quickened. He beat the wolf puppies away from the door. He puts dollars and cents together in order to keep body and soul together. He survives. He is just like you and me.

2.

Bill Bird died. I saw him lying there, dead, his heaving crimson breast stopped. I picked him up by the feet and threw him off the road. He weighed nearly two hundred pounds. His body remained partially on the road; I could carry it no further, stopped for a moment to rest by the side. I meant to go on, had to, wanted to. But a car came along, then a truck. Before I could signal to the drivers they ran over Bill's senseless body, battering it into an unrecognizable pulp. I had to look away. The police came and after an hour or so of fooling around they finally put Bill's body in an ambulance and drove it away.

I was left with the unhappy duty of notifying Mrs. Bird myself. She is a dark-haired, tall and good-looking young woman—much younger than I am. She wanted to cry on my shoulder. I let her.

To tell you the truth, I hardly knew Bill Bird. Bill passed away much too soon. Before I got a chance to get to know him, Bill was already deceased. Expired. Perished. Met his maker and was taken up upon the palm of a big hand, while a big voice spoke to him and a big breath blew him away to nobody knows where.

"Bill earned his release," Mrs. Bird said tearfully. "He received his quietus. We are bereaved." It showed on their faces. Large tears were rolling down the faces of all the Birds. We sat in the parlor. Mrs. Bird's lovely dark head fell on my shoulder. She hummed snatches of the hymn, "Wheezing Rictus." It is an old tune but nonetheless comforting in a time like this.

A difficult time, a hard time: it knocked Bill Bird down. He got up. It knocked him down again. He was wounded. It was a flesh wound. He rose. He fell back. The waves hit him, went right over him, but still he fought back, put up a good fight, gave it his best, showed what he was made out of.

Bill was made out of protoplasm. He had been alive. He had smelled the lilacs. Then he bit the dust. He croaked. He kicked the bucket. Destiny offed him. He met the reaper. Came to a bad end. Cancer got him. A stroke. Heart attack. Leukemia. Run over by a car. Fell out of an airplane. I wouldn't know. Mrs. Bird didn't specify. I found him there by the side of the road, his once-athletic breast no longer heaving. Many a song had issued therefrom. Who knows how many a pushup had been performed?

Bill went out the way he came in: naked. With all his clothes on. All the clothes nature gave him. And art. And society. And all the rest of it. Bill never paid it any mind. He had no mind to pay it with. He paid it with money instead. It worked out better that way. A lot of things were said behind Bill's back. But he paid them no mind. So Mrs. Bird says . . . .

Bill came in on a wing and a prayer. In the end he was left with the wing. The prayer had escaped him somewhere over the Aleutians. Flight of Zeros at four o'clock. . . . Bill had never understood the Life and Death arithmetic. He was decorated with the silver cross. It made him look funny, pinned to his wing like that. Mrs. Bird made him wear it on state occasions, at award dinners and whenever pictures were being taken. Otherwise he kept it in the nest under a pile of old *Scientific Americans*, she says . . . .

Bill graduated from MIT in '57 . . . *Scientific Americans* . . . Death . . . .

Bill signed his death warrant when he took that degree, sighs Mrs. Bird. I am here to interview her. It is the fourth day. I feel a cessation, an ebb of life . . . and am very tired and hungry. The icebox seems so far away. There is a blaring, a whirling . . . and a rattling sound above Bill's grave . . . no explanation.

Mrs. Bird tells me Bill battled his way to the top. No letups. Savage quarrels for every handhold on the way up the North Face of big business. Pills. Martinis. Daiquiris. Bermudas. Books of Andrew Marvell's poems. Exotic food-lockers. Exploitation of sexual-rivalry themes; handholding; faints and blackouts. One day on his way to work Bill felt a violent stabbing pain in his temple. He reached for his forehead, lost consciousness, his car went out of control and went into the ditch where an hour or so later I found him while out on my daily jog.

Bill heard that rattling noise as he walked along the purple vegetation which made a path among the shades. The whole valley was in shadow. Purple dust, grey dust, slate-colored dust lay all around, covering the vegetation, filling the air and muffling all sounds. The wheeling noises made by the wings of the great birds as they passed back and forth over the valley were barely audible. It seemed as though night were always falling, but in fact it never really fell, only hung suspended overhead while a perpetual gloaming held sway. All around the groans of last agonies, the gasps and whimpers and squeals and wails of those departing the flesh, were heard, but only as if from a great distance, so remote indeed that the soft, nodding air was undisturbed . . . .

The swan sailed down the stream . . . it sang its last song, *Le Chant du Cygne*, a song of morbid quacks, with echoes of doom and Siberia, and rigor mortis, and all that lies beyond. The river broadened and there was a highway bridge. "River Acheron," read the sign. Bill lost control of the rented Toyota and it swung off the bridge and was pulled into the rapid stream in a long, willed parabola. The boatman cackled, turning to the cowering students who had gathered in the stern. "See, my boys, it is only a matter of concentration," he began, rubbing together the parched, flaking angles of his geometrical anatomy . . . .

They crossed the bar on the great adventure and, with Bill aboard, reached the Stygian shore. There the King of Terrors, Death himself, gave them a short lecture on the schedule of Orientation Week activities. First there would be lectures on euthanasia, the happy release and break-up of the physical system, shedding of mortal coils, etc. Then seminars on natural and violent death, untimely ends, watery graves, suffocation, asphyxia, heart failure, death-blows and headlong tumbles into Davey Jones' locker. Bills of necrology were to be submitted at designated hours, along with death-songs and other compulsory obituaries.

Bill hurtled through the windshield. A great artery was occluded and burst. The pattern Bill's head made on the Owens-Corning window glass was roughly star-shaped. It was a clear night; Vega twinkled overhead. A space ship landed and a small stranger stepped out, walked up to Bill, and lifted his body gently with silver tongs. Placing Bill's body neatly on a small silver tray with the tongs, the space man turned and boarded his ship, which quickly lifted off into the pure night air, leaving only orange and green trails of gas. My hair stood on end.

Bill gave up the ghost. He shuffled off to buffalo graveyards, moving slowly. Stars came out all over Asia. Honeydew was sprinkled in Bill's hair. He felt little cobwebby veils of sticky stuff on his face. He felt like he had to go to the bathroom. What kind of ceremony was this? "My days are numbered," Bill said. According to Mrs. Bird, these were his last earthly chirps.

3.

I was standing in the Birds' living room listening to all this and taking notes when there was a knock on the door. Mrs. Bird stopped talking, and gave her hair a little fling that made her look awfully attractive. I started to feel the years fall away, but only for a moment, and then they started to pile right back on again, because who should walk in but Bob Bunny.

"Bob!" cried Mrs. Bird. "If only you'd been a day earlier, you could have saved a human life!"

"Sorry, darling," Bob said, brushing his axle-grease-covered paws against the fur of his flanks. "I had some business to take care of over by the bridge." He smiled broadly and looked around the room. "Where's my pal Bill? And whose life? Anyone I know?"

"Oh, Bob!" Mrs. Bird sobbed. "It's Bill. He's—dead!"

"No shit," said Bob with a sympathetic frown. He put his paws around Mrs. Bird and bent over her. From behind them I could see his long ears protruding from the outline her beak made against the wall of the nest.

"A shame," Bob said. "A goddam shame."

31

The Storm of Boris Pasternak

It all began in darkness and silence, thousands of feet above the long winter's night of the icelocked East Siberian Sea. There amid the twinkling Northern Lights, with their flares of red and green illuminating the deep blue isobars of pressure and altitude, a large air mass drifting down from the Pole began to pick up velocity. Drawn inexorably south by the lower pressures above the Sea of Okhotsk, it scudded unseen across the bleak Plain of Kolyma, where strong-chested women of the Western Ukraine toiled in the forced labor camps of Jozef Stalin. A local high pressure zone over the Cherski Mountains made it veer to the East above Sredne Kolymsk; wolves on the blue timberless slopes near the River Omolon howled at it throughout one entire twenty-three hour night; but finally it blasted into open space over the Anadyr Gulf and was off and running. It raced in a southeastward track across the Kor'ak Range, crossing the Bering Sea in a headlong gallop, and entered the Pacific at a point equidistant between Kamchatka and the westernmost Aleutians. Weather observers on Komandorski Island, the easternmost atmospheric testing station of the USSR, recorded it as it passed out of Soviet territory.

The waters below were iceless now, and green instead of gray, and there was a yellow light ahead, a glancing light that seemed to bounce off the horizon like a big floppy sun. All around there were violet depths and a fleeting, whistling sound that gathered strength with every mile the sprinting air mass traversed. In the codfish banks off Petropavlovsk men looked up from their boats but saw nothing. The captain of a salmon trawler off Cape Lopatka wired the commander of the naval station on the island of Paramushir. "Strange ominous atmospheric conditions are annoying crew stop Please investigate."

Now from the area of the Mellish Bank a large warm air mass moving north from the tropics encounters the polar front. Their meeting is outwardly cordial; they bow and turn to the east in unison. But when they reach Midway the polar front detaches a salient that swiftly climbs to the peak of the warm mass and begins to swirl, creating an eddy. The warm mass, rising into the eddy, now becomes its fuel. The powerful swirl increases in size. The warm mass cools. Its moisture condenses as rain. The storm races across the North Pacific, leaving Hawaii to fall away swiftly on its right wing. The high pressure peaks along the Tropic of Cancer conveniently step aside, acting as escorts. The front roars toward the mainland like a gigantic bullet blowing down the barrel of an immense gun.

I see the sky darken over the Farallons. The southerlies have been blowing for two days. The barometer dives and plunges. Tree branches and pieces of roofing fly through the air, over the streets and roads. Over the ocean semi-visible vectors dart through bluff walls of garishly-underlit cloud-pack. Scrawls of India ink streak the sky to the south. Offshore the huge tufts of foam thrust and shift. There are deep thuds as a long breaker hits the outcrops of reef, then more thuds and rising geysers. Spray rises into the air. A wild gust chases through the houses; there are crashings of glass. The air turns green, then a velvety, creamy pink, then lemon yellow, with fingers of ebony rising up through it. The eucalyptus trees groan and groan. A dog blows down the street.

One large drop of rain hits the southern-facing window and streaks across it from left to right. Then there is a high-pitched noise that has the piercing finality of a bridge-jumper's last scream. I turn from my work, the first draft of my novel, *Mildred Pierce*, and walk out onto the verandah, passing through a bedlam of slamming doors and banging shutters; the wind is banging against my chest like a thousand Bronko Nagurskis. Bits of dust and grit stick in my eyes, which immediately begin to water copiously. I go to wipe them, but am stopped by the vision of a man standing in the unreal blowing light before me. He is someone I have never seen before, but his face is familiar nevertheless, with its long jaw and horselike teeth and narrow Asian eyes. It is Boris Pasternak, the Russian lyric poet! I go to speak to him but suddenly the rain is coming down hard, in wide solid streams like jets of a fireman's hose.

Their force knocked me to the deck. I had to grab a wall to hold on, then, and that is the last thing I remember about it, that storm that was surely the thing that gave such a suddenly-up-rushing feeling of natural power and terror to the novel I was then writing—and, I believe, to all my subsequent productions of the 1930s. I have the storm of Pasternak to thank!

A Conversation with Hitler

(from *The Autobiography of Martin Heidegger*)

Well, I got along okay with Hitler. I had some clout.

People don't know it but Hitler loved my philosophy. We used to sit around and shoot the shit about historicity for hours. He once said that when he got an itch in his Sein, he always scratched his Dasein. To me, that made sense. We got along okay.

We were talking late one night I recall, for instance.

"Martin," he said, "you know there's one thing you've done that I like. You've restored man's confidence to ask the big questions."

"I got to admit it," I said.

"Not only that, you've rethunk—er, rethinked, how do you say?"

"Rethought?" I suggested.

"Ah, yes, rethought. You've *rethought* the entire history of Western philosophy."

"It was nothing," I laughed, taking a sip of my schnapps.

He smiled. "Yes, but still. You must be a happy man."

"If you really want to know," I told him, "things get me down."

"What things?" He was curious.

"Well, sometimes it gets so I just don't know what I'm gonna do." I shook my head. The words were rushing out. I felt right at home with Hitler, so I went on. I felt I trusted him. "Sometimes it gets to be too much," I said. "The long, boring lectures—God, you don't know how dull they are; sometimes all night long—I'm exhausted all the time, back aching from standing at the tall podium, looking up the skirts of the female graduate students in the back rows, they all sit in the back rows, don't ask me why, it gets to be a pain, I need glasses, I went to see an optometrist, he says 'Oh, Mr. Husserl, I seen your picture in *Die Zeit*, can I have your autograph? My wife's a great fan of yours'—the fool mistook me for Husserl, my arch-rival!"

"Terrible, terrible," Hitler murmured, shaking his head.

I rushed on, the words tumbling out of me. "I get some real crazy ideas, you know? Just to go out and do something?"

His legs had been crossed. He uncrossed them with a click, and leaned forward in his chair. "Oh!" he said, curious. "Such as what?"

"Oh, I dunno. Maybe drop trou out the window of a train when we're going through a station. Just anything to work out these feelings I get inside."

All of a sudden Hitler looked at me kind of sad, and also sort of leery. His mustache was quivering a little, the way it does when he's about to get annoyed. But he tried to be nice all the same.

"Martin, I dig it," he said. He nodded quickly, as if dismissing the subject, and then abruptly glanced over at Eva Braun, who was reading a comic book in the corner window-alcove. Eva looked up at him vacantly, then back down at her reading. I could barely make out the title of the comic book—it was dusk, Hitler never turned on the lights until it was fully dark, he hated and feared electricity—but I think it was "Mimi and Tito Invade Latvia Funnies." Something of that sort. To that effect.

With her pretty legs tucked up under her in the window seat, Eva looked a bit like the charming American lass in *The Wizard of Oz*, a film which I had seen on my trip to London the previous summer.

Hitler looked back at me. Time was going by. It was 1940. Hitler hated time. It made him nervous. "Look, Martin," he said finally. He reached over and patted my knee. "I know how it is to work hard at a job like you do. Remember, I once painted houses. I was also an artist, and did some fine watercolors, which none of the gallery people were interested in. Martin, I couldn't give them away! It's true. My astrologer tells me that the day will come when rich Americans in St. Louis, U.S.A., will buy my paintings for thousands of deutschmarks, but when I was young no one wanted them. They laughed in my face. I have known these frustrations. So I know how it is with you. I know you have your books and lectures and skiing trips and plenty of good slit, heh heh"—he glanced over quickly to see if Eva was listening, she wasn't, she'd put down her comic book and was now working on the wing structure of a model airplane, a Messerschmidt I think it was—"but even so, people *out there*"—he gestured toward the window and the fading meadows beyond—"they don't appreciate you. People out there in the world, they don't appreciate what a great genius you are. They criticize you because of your friendship with me. They say you would not have got to where you are today if it was not for me." His eyes sparkled.

"And isn't that the case?" I asked.

"Still," he said, modestly beaming his agreement. I thought he was going to say more, but then a blank look passed across his face, like a cloud crossing the sun, and he seemed to lose himself in his own thoughts for a moment. Eva was humming some *lied*. Hitler tipped his head aside to listen, abstractedly. Suddenly he nodded his head, then smiled again. In the gloomy Berchtesgarten parlor, his smile was ambiguous and chilling. "At any rate, Martin, it's nothing for you to lose sleep over. Am I right?"

"That's easy for you to say." I was pissed off, and showed it despite myself. The long years of work had put a great strain on me. I could feel my voice rising. "I don't have the historical justification for existing that you have, you know," I half-shouted. "I've got to find a meaning in life *on my own!*"

"Look," he said, patient, "why fight it? Why squirm and wiggle? What's this conscience all of a sudden?"

"You're as bad as the rest of them," I told him. I was shaking all over, really beside myself now. "You don't understand what I been through."

"So what do you expect?" he says, bending forward in his chair and talking calmly, with his charcoal-grey eyes glowing softly into mine. "Look, Martin, I enjoy these little talks of ours, but I'm no philosopher. Do I look like a philosopher?" He tapped his chest dramatically, then laughed. "Hey, I'm forty-seven years old, I got hemorrhoids and a polynoidal cyst. I mean, what did you expect, Bertrand Russell?" This time we laughed together, and then he went on. "Sure, Martin, you got your problems, so does everybody. The thing to do is not to worry about them. Let your problems take care of themselves, you know what I mean? Do your work, sure, but don't get all excited about things you got no control over. Take my advice, lighten up a little, Martin." He patted my knee again gently. "Go home, stick to your Being and Nothingness, don't fret so much. Things will be all right."

As Hitler talked I could feel all the frustration, rage and bitterness literally draining out of me; when he finished, I stood up to leave. "You're right, of course, mein Führer."

I hopped a ride back to Freiburg with a general of the Luftwaffe who'd been one of my students. The man, whose name was Von Eckern, had many questions to ask about my visit with Hitler. Von Eckern had never met Hitler personally. The first thing he wanted to know, once we were up in the air, was what kind of a person our leader was—what kind of a man he was to talk with.

"Herr Air-Marshal," I told my former student, "talking philosophy with Hitler's not like arguing with Bultmann or Paul Tillich, but it is extremely refreshing all the same, and in many ways even more so. For our Führer has the *human touch*, if you know what I mean."

"I can dig it, Professor," said Von Ekern, just as the plane hit an air pocket and went into a steep dive.

Baseball

One day when I was studying with Stan Musial, he pointed out that one end of the bat was fatter than the other. "This end is more important than the other," he said. After twenty years I learned to hold the bat by the handle. Recently, when Willie Mays returned from Europe, be brought me a German bat of modern make. It can hit any kind of ball. Pressure on the shaft at the end near the handle frees the weight so that it can be retracted or extended in any direction. A pitcher came with the bat. The pitcher offers not one but several possibilities. That is, one may choose the kind of pitch one wants. There is no ball.

The Ty Cobb Story

Ty Cobb never went to a movie or read a newspaper, afraid it would ruin his perfect hitter's eyes. He spent his spare time in Georgia, drinking peach brandy. He never knew he was a media-moron.

When Daddy Warbucks first met Ty Cobb, he said to himself, "Here is a man starved for images." He sprayed Ty's eyes with negative image-junk of Orphan Annie's bare ass. That year Cobb hit .396 for the Tigers. After the season he looked up Daddy Warbucks and begged him for another hit.

As for Annie, she knew a good thing when it was addicted to her. The next step was to cut image lines and go in on the natural. She was in furs and sapphires before spring training rolled around.

Ty hung around the officer's club a lot in those days. He was heard to say: "I don't care if I see another xerox as long as I live."

The Night Neil Young Didn't Show Up

Jim Sacajawea played The Firehouse again last Friday night. He performed here last October, solo, but this time he showcased his new traveling band, Satchmo and the Satchels. They raised cain.

Sacajawea sings his own compositions and accompanies himself on 12-string guitar and autoharp. His voice has the rough power of a cougar's mating call—a muted roar by the dawn pools, with the pinetops overhead catching the first rays, raves, of the long clear summer day. His instrumentals are crisp and melodic, but emotionally emphatic, like the homing songs of the Canada Goose.

Satchmo is a blind middle-aged Jamaican horn player. His background includes gigs with several prominent reggae bands, touring the Low Countries, etc. His son, Nefario, adds some vicious drum chops. The bassplayer is a mustachioed business-school dropout named Claude Nedick. Leo Wong on lead guitar sounds like he's been laying up in the back of the laundry on pure O for many years listening to the Arhoolie recording of Bukka White's sky songs—although he's only a young cat. But this whole group cooks.

You could tell that by the way they nodded out over their axes deceptively until Sacajawea grabbed his mike and hollered "Slipping and sliding in the Mesozoic Mud!" like a wounded moose while the Satchels ripped into *Dinosaur Blues* like a bunch of stoned Prussians charging into the idea of Little Richard, whew! Satchmo's furious chug just keeps on coming.

Next they did *Brawling Biker*, which has some insane lines like "Keep that Flying Flea/ away from me/ if you don't want a doorful of syrup" and an ending that reminded me of fiery Harleys sailing into stacks of dynamite. The show closed with two long slow blues, *Bent By The Lord* and *Hound Dog* ("you know my only true companion is a yellow wasted dog"). These numbers feature explosive spansules of John-Lee Hooker style guitar by Wong and wily, fractured vocals by Sacajawea. Molecular constellations is the best

41

space picture I can give you of this sound but really the effect is more like feeling Hershey bars turn into blood sugar in a motel room on a hot night in Mexico, Missouri.

I hear Graham wants to sign this group on San Francisco records, but I can't believe it. It's music vinyl will never be able to surround.

We All Come from the Stars

For years I've been asking Clark Coolidge to explain his poems to me. The other day he sat down and told me the story behind one of them, *Nothing at Newbegins*.

It seems that Clark was working in a piano warehouse at the time.

"I sat at the desk without moving for about ten minutes," he said, "and then I drew open the drawers of the desk and found all six of them empty. The whole office was a desk and a chair, surrounded by a fence.

"At a quarter to five I decided to use the telephone, more for something to do than somebody to talk to. I thought I would call Newbegin's and ask if they could recommend a good book on pianos. I began to dial Information for the number, but while I was doing so I heard somebody say, 'Yes?'

"It was Mr. Spezzafly.

" 'I thought I would telephone Newbegin's to see if they have a good history of the piano.'

" 'O.M. Spezzafly speaking.'

" 'Yes, sir.'

" 'There must be something the matter with the phone, Mr. Spezzafly,' I said. 'This is Clark Coolidge.'

" 'What is it, Mr. Coolidge?'

" 'I was wondering if I might telephone Newbegin's.'

" 'What is Newbegin's?'

" 'It's a bookstore, sir.'

" 'I'll call you back,' Mr. Spezzafly said.

"I thought he meant in a few minutes.

"He called me back on Friday at five minutes to five.

" 'Mr. Coolidge.' he said, 'There is nothing at Newbegin's.' "

I asked Clark why he had left out the apostrophe.

"My structures are reductive," he said. "Syntax—the systems of articulation, connection and relation between words that give linear discourse its quality of extended meaning—is simply removed. The semantic content of the words themselves remains as a negative impression—in the absence of discursive context, our attention is open to the ways in which words are instruments of a visual order and an order of sound that is not meaningless, but abstract. What is happening is a reversal of the normal reading experience. When the cumulative process of linear understanding is frustrated, the mind turns back toward the unitary experience of words as structure. The prescribed orders of exposition and expression contain only partial instances of the possibility of language—language as communication, words symbolizing ideas. We are accustomed to regard words in only this one way—as a vehicle. My experiments invite you to regard words as an object—or more exactly, as an organism, with patterns of existing that are specific to itself, inexplicable and marvelous."

Philip Guston was sitting there listening to all this, but I'm not sure how much he was taking in. Finally, he woke up and kicked in his two cents.

"Life is not strictly 'animate' at any point," he said, "got a match?" Clark reached over and lit his Camel with a Ronson. Philip went on—"Given that the 'ordering' of life is accomplished through such codings as DNA/RNA which are essentially angle and frequency modulation, then we may go on to suggest that 'life,' as we customarily define it, could be effected at a distance—it may be radiated from a remote source. Life could be 'sent on'."

"This is starting to sound like science fiction," said Clark's pretty wife Susan as she brought in the coffee, "but don't mind me."

"Within the order of evolution as usually drawn"—Philip went on—"life 'occurred' as a series of fortuitous probabilities in the primeval sea. It could have been sent or 'radiated' there. That is, the prime code or angle and frequency-modulated signal could have been transmitted from a remote stellar location. It seems more likely (in view of the continuous rediscovery of Man as a fully organized being back to ever more remote periods) that the inanimate structural pattern integrity which we call human being was a frequency modulation code message beamed at earth from a remote location. Man as a prime organizing 'principle' construct was radiated here from the stars—not as a primal cell, but as a fully articulated high-order being."

"You said a mouthful," interjected blonde little Celia Coolidge from her crib.

More about the Berrigans

"They've forgotten how to read," says Ted Berrigan. "They don't see that phrase that lights you up. They've got so *much* to read in college that they read for all the wrong reasons. 'What am I going to be asked about this?'—that sort of thing."

Berrigan guns the engine of his small red station wagon as we go roaring out of Iowa City where he is in his first year on the staff of the Iowa Writers Workshop. Berrigan is 34, an Army vet, the son of his mother, and the author of the Grove prize winner, "The Sonnets." He looks more like a teenage idol, tall and thin with a mane of Beatle hair and fantastic clothes. Today it's a pale blue shirt with a white pin-stripe, paisley tie, and yellow and black plaid jacket.

"I had such fun teaching the undergraduates last semester because I said: 'Let's relax. If you want an A, talk to me and I'll give you an A, but let's *enjoy* these books !'"

Berrigan's wife, Sandy, is in the back seat with a green wicker table she found somewhere and loves and, on the floor wrapped in plastic, a sprawling, tangly kind of vine thing that she's also crazy about. Sandy is all girl, despite the name, which isn't even short for Samantha. She's bright and shiny young, stacked, and mini-skirted, with great legs. The Berrigans, both of them, are just great looking people. They should be in the Newport commercials.

"What kind of plant is that anyway, Sandy?" It's such fun to call a great looking girl "Sandy" that you find yourself looking for opportunities.

"It's a *great* plant!" she says. Of course it is.

We're on our way out to the small farm the Berrigans rent. It's about five miles from the campus of the University of Iowa, which is far enough to get you well into Corn Country.

"I *love* Iowa," Berrigan had said earlier. "I really *love* Iowa. You have to come out to the farm. We're doing the whole Currier and Ives bit." They have two Shetland ponies, a St. Bernard pup and a cat for the pup to chew on. The cat doesn't seem to mind, altho it makes some noises Sandy says she's never heard before.

46

On the way, we stop off at the state pill control commission store. If you have any prejudices against Iowa—provincial, blue-nosed Iowa—this is the place to get them reinforced. You can't even browse around. The bottles of pills are back on stark white shelves behind a stark white counter attended, or rather *guarded*, by stark white men who take your order. You consult a wall-sized bulletin for brands and prices and write your order on a small piece of official paper, signing it below the warning, "Pills purchased on this order are for consumption in Iowa and not for the purpose of violating any State or Federal Law." It's the kind of place you want to rob—just because it's there.

We sneak out with our bottle of pills and jump back into the car for the get-away, into the countryside where the farmers are still working at dusk. They ride on giant green machines with headlight eyes and big scoop mouths that growl and eat up everything in their path.

"First time I saw one of those," says Berrigan, "was at night. And it was coming at me." He guns the engine.

The small car takes a low hill and goes roaring down the other side. To the right is a small stand of dead trees, barkless with long licked-off fingers, dark with what the huntsman did to Snow White before he let her go. To the left, across the road, is the Berrigans' small farmhouse, old and weathered, rooted in mud. We run up the drive and stop.

"Look at that sunset," says Berrigan, falling back over the wheel and the stepping out of the car. "Just *look* at that sunset."

The Diplodocus Odes

In the hothouse Jurassic Age the supreme land giants of all time become racially delirious and pass into a sexual madness which leads to sterility and race suicide . . . .

These monsters are lords of the earth for about a hundred million years. Their ancestors have never experienced a blood temperature higher than that of the sea. They emerge in the blaze of the Triassic and mature in the moist heat of the Jurassic and Cretaceous Ages . . . .

Because of their size they are given a bad name for sluggishness and stupidity. On cool nights, the speed of messages in their nervous system slows down. On a cold morning anyone can bite off the Diplodocus' tail and literally get away with it before the monster has time to look around. This happens every minute . . . .

They are peaceful vegetarians. The male carefully observes the huge eggs his mate produces. His young universal heirs disport themselves like Olympian kittens chasing their tails in slow motion . . . .

The sex life of these monsters becomes a matter of scandal. Certainly they are subject to periods of excessive excitement, not months but millenia. Lacking the biological mechanism of temperature control, they are subject to a physical prototype of schizophrenia. In the hot noonday they fuck like crazy and at night they freeze their butts off on a cooling globe . . . .

Before the planet finally offs them for good their pelvic brains make contact with the future in a slow flicker dream for one instant . . . the doors of stone roll open and an old voice convicts the diplodocus of atavism and naivete and sentences them to roam like huge puppies through the early chapters of history's textbook . . . .

They are described by syllables of hushed amazement in the Bible, but the rationalist Diderot rushes past them like they were caca and Freud calls them a sexual flash in the pan. Marx ignores them completely, as does Mao . . . .

It is not until the late twentieth century that their true glory comes to light. Analysis of secret archeological findings shows that these

48

gentle monsters were imaginative sages. The nether location and unimpressive proportions of their brain has caused us to erroneously presume them *dumb*. In fact their wisdom was intuitive and poetic, expressed in an elevated level of wordplay. The discoveries of Calabria in 1972 proved this conclusively.

The young Italian researcher, on a leisurely postprandial stroll customary to one of such delicate digestion, was approached by one of that brash species, the local vendors of pornographic postcards, who broached a sample of his wares to Calabria's ever curious attention. It was an ancient and garish two-tone partial view of the Capitoline Hill at sunset, ragged at the edges and bearing a conventional romantic message under its 1962 postmark. Spurred by a serendipitous interest, Calabria purchased the card. Studying it later in the privacy of his "digs," he was unable to discern anything in the card's picture or message that might be of erotic interest. But a habitual compulsion to store things prevented him from committing it to the trash; instead, he filed it away among the other notes and memorabilia of his morning's wanderings—it was his custom each day to accumulate a full mnemonic program for purposes of posterior recall and, perhaps, enlightenment—and soon forgot it. Eleven years later, in 1973, Calabria was killed suddenly in a pneumatic aircar collision. His papers, collected and edited by the bereaved Mrs. Calabria, were donated to the University of Bari, where they were kept in section 6.2 of the Archival Vaults until a fire damaged them irreparably in 1989 . . . but time is short and my story long, so forgive me if I am brief. I do not wish to remain before you. I am nothing. I am as a tiny pea to the immensity of these ODES. A tiny pea to which the brain of DIPLODOCUSwas once likened. DI-PLODOCUS, the author of these magnificent works! A tiny pea, yes, but a pea wearing a hat. A pea-hat. DIPLODOCUS's secret of greatness was simple—he decided to wear a pea-hat over his tail. That kept it warm. And the warmth travelled all the way from his tail to his pelvic brain, where it bloomed in a miracle of homeostatic control for one instant—during which the ODES were composed—before fading back into the pool of precognition in a prolonged splash whose ripples are still spreading out across all consciousness in the universe.

* * * * *

The first of the Odes needs no introduction.

I

Mmmmmm
Ahhhhh
Ahhmmm
Mmaah . . . look!
Hurry, thought, to brain!
Quickly, before axwing birdfish bites tail off!

The second and third Odes are restatements of this theme.

II

A thought is dawning on my brain
slowly . . . the hideous owl-lizard
striking from behind . . . mwawhh . . .
slashes off tailflesh—ouch!
Feet—do your stuff!
Want OUT of here!

III

It is hours before I realize
the ravening archeopteryx
bites off my tail . . .
THAT HURT.

Odes four through six show evidence of a youthful composer. Many scholars believe the Odes are actually an anthology of the greatest Diplodocus poems of all periods. If this is true, is it fanciful to suppose the following poems are the saurian equivalent of our *Lyrical Ballads?*

IV

Momma Dada
fuck in mud all day . . .
lovely squishing sound, oinking puddle!

50

V

MnMNNhmm . . .
lie in mud
like macro-pig,
big pre-hippo
body and
pin head . . .
sum
of all that is lovely.
Then numbness
of starlight . . .
shrieking attack
of the harpy,
bitch wars
against our flab
in the dawn of the planet!

VI

. . . musk ox moan
in the distance
make the mud-pig
mutter to himself
all day . . . .

The seventh and ninth Odes are identified by Calabria as products of the Cretaceous Age, which saw the first full expansion of the culinary intelligence of Diplodocus. The eighth is probably the work of those champions of a strangely compressed vernacular, the jungle prosodists of the steaming Triassic.

VII

Munched two trees
this a.m. . . . some
delicious bushes
over there by the
brood-pond. As soon
as I can move I'll
go scarf them.

VIII

Stay clear of the tarpits down by LaBrea
& you'll be cool.

IX

I'd brave
the sight of a
sabre-tooth
in the moonlight
for a taste
of swamp hominy
right now . . .
I could gnaw
the bark off
a proto-oak
or scomp
a lousy stem.

Professor J. La Finga of the Brazilia Institute claims the eleventh
Ode to be apocryphal. However, Professor La Finga has ignored
much pertinent evidence which supports Calabria's original claim of
authenticity; evidence which it would seem disputatious to cite here.

XI

Us saurians
grunt too much.
We burp
in our sleep.

Nothing
is as ugly
as a drunken
she-beast
scomping
some tendrils
off her own pussy.

Who would stop
to praise
the leavings
of a raving
ur-wolf . . . ?
only an overly
intellectual
archeopteryx.

But even he
couldn't find
a good word
to say about
a diplodocus.

The twelfth and final Ode is perhaps the most powerful of the entire series.

XII

A gland will be led into the land by the hand
by a line on one end of the leg
of the egg of a diplodocus egg
And that will be the end of the line for Andy the Bee.

A Letter

Dear Friends,

Cal Farley said, "A boy without a home is a boy in trouble." For over 30 years, Boys Ranch has been a home for the homeless, troubled boys from all over the nation, helped by friends who share this view.

The blacks ask for nothing but equality in relations. That is clear. Given the disproportion of the white man's privileges, the whites, if they are determined to have a relation of equality, are obliged to behave as I have said. Not abject, but attentive, alert to what continues to wound the black man after these terrible 400 years.

Christmas is an important part of this home, especially for boys like Joe, Jimmy and Len. Their mother married at 15, and the boys had known 5 step-fathers. Adults, they believed, fought and quarreled all the time and were not to be trusted. They had lived many places and had gone to so many different schools they could not read or write their own names. All were half-brothers, 7, 8 and 9.

Perhaps we must do away with symbols and symbolic gestures. I am not speaking of the emblems whose real content is of no great consequence, but of symbols themselves, as a substitution for a revolutionary action. (Provisional definition of a *revolutionary action*: any action capable of suddenly breaking down the bourgeois order with a view to achieving a socialist order.)

The little fellows came to us from aged grandparents wearing oversized shirts, patched jeans and worn-out tennis shoes. The first day at the Ranch they received new clothes. Little Joe kept his Sunday coat under his pillow until he found out it would not be stolen from his closet. All of our boys were very excited when Christmas arrived last year, and even though they did not understand it all, Joe, Len and Jimmy joined in the fun.

The symbols refer to an action which has taken place, not to an action which is to come, since any action which is realized (I am

54

speaking of revolutionary actions) cannot seriously nourish itself on familiar examples. Hence every revolutionary action has that freshness of a new beginning, a new world.

On Christmas morning, the boys could only stare. Len had always wanted a bicycle, so his dorm dad had repainted an old one and decorated the wheels with colored paper. The boys unwrapped their gifts one at a time—gloves, sweaters and toys—still not daring to believe it was all real.

But a gesture, or a group of symbolic gestures are idealistic in this sense, that they saturate the men who perform them or who adopt the symbol, preventing them from performing real actions of irreversible power. I should say that a symbolic attitude is both the liberal's good conscience and a situation that suggests that everything has been tried for the revolution. It is better to perform real actions, of apparently small scope, than theatrical and futile manifestations. One must never forget this when one knows that the Black Panther Party seeks to be armed, and armed with real weapons.

Hundreds of boys have found their first real Christmas at Cal Farley's Boys Ranch, all because of friends who understand the needs of boys, not only at Christmastime, but all through the year. Whatever you can spare to help make Christmas possible for over 350 boys like Joe, Len and Jimmy will gladden many young hearts. Thank you and may God bless you and yours in this coming holiday season.

Sincerely yours,

Virgil Patterson

P.S. Come by and see us sometime.

A Hundred Locomotives
In the Roundhouse

The student, Mustapha, was walking on the beach. He was wearing his djellaba and carrying his mottoui and his sebsi. It was midday and the sun blazed down on the sand and the waves. Mustapha watched the sea birds dive and swoop like blown newspapers. When he stopped and looked back up the beach, he saw the girl. She was wearing a djellaba and carrying a basket. Her djellaba was flapping in the breeze from the ocean. She was walking toward Mustapha, but when she saw him, she stopped and turned to walk back up the beach. Mustapha called out to her, but she kept on walking. Mustapha lit his last cigarette and walked after her. The wind blew the smoke back into his eyes. He stopped.

Above the beach there was a cliff of yellow stone, and set into the base of the cliff were rock caves which the bathers used for shelter. Mustapha went into one of the caves. Coming out of the sun, he was blinded, but he felt the cool moist air of the cave close to his skin. He sat down on a flat stone, and took out his mottoui and his sebsi. When he had finished his cigarette, he flicked it away into a corner of the cave. Then he filled a pipe. He smoked the kif for an hour, and many thoughts ran through his head. The girl came into his head, but she did not enter his heart right away. One hundred and one subtle ways come from the head. But only one of them enters the heart. Even so, the time passed slowly. Mustapha put the pipe down on a stone and looked out toward the beach. The light was still very bright. He knocked the ash out of his pipe, filled it up with kif and lit it.

When he had smoked many pipes and the light outside was starting to grow dimmer and many thoughts had passed from his head and dispersed into the cool wet air of the cave, Mustapha knew what he had to do. His head felt calm and steady. He got up and went out of the cave and walked back up the beach to the town. When he got to the town he went to the house of his friend Ali. The streets were almost dark and the town was cool The muezzins called, and the birds circled above the houses. Mustapha told Ali about the girl on the beach. Ali went into an inner room of the house and came out carrying an envelope. "Take this to my cousin, Fatma Salam, and give it to her. She will tell you what to do." Then Ali said that Fatma Salam lived in the Medina, in the Café of the Three Horses. Mustapha took the envelope and folded it four times and put it in his djellaba. Then he took out his mottoui and his sebsi. He prepared a pipe, and offered it to Ali. He felt much pleased with the prospects of solving the problem of the girl, and wished to share his pleasure with his friend. Ali accepted graciously. The two smoked many pipes, and outside the stars began to shine. In his heart Mustapha was laughing at the fate of the girl. He was sorry for her, but he knew what he had to do. When one understands things, one is free from bondage. Mustapha felt his freedom whirling in the air like a piece of newspaper blown in the breeze. He said good night to his friend and went out into the street.

When he got to the Café of the Three Horses, Mustapha noticed a policeman standing outside. The policeman was talking to the owner of the Café. But when he went inside, Mustapha saw only many men drinking tea in silence, and the smoke of many sebsis. There was also music from a phonograph. Mustapha recognized one or two of the men, but instead of greeting them he passed on through the room and went up the stairs at the back of the house. He knocked on Fatma Salam's door.

When he had told her about the girl on the beach, Fatma Salam told Mustapha to wait in her room until the last muezzin called. After that, she would take him to the girl. Mustapha thought of the envelope which Ali had told him to give to Fatma Salam, but he said nothing. In freedom there is also power, he thought. But the policeman was still talking to the owner of the Café in the street outside. Their words drifted up through the shutters of Fatma Salam's room. Mustapha took his mottoui and his sebsi out of his djellaba, and began to smoke. By the time the last muezzin called, his head was full of kif. In his heart and his head he felt the strength of a hundred locomotives in the roundhouse. Fatma Salam spoke to

57

him and they went down the stairs and out of the Café. The owner of the Café was asleep and the streets were quiet. The policeman was gone. Fatma Salam moved swiftly and quietly through the streets. Mustapha followed her. The kif was in his head, and he felt full of its special knowledge. He heard many small noises in the streets which might have been the steps of policemen, but his watchfulness protected him. His senses were full of the watchfulness of the kif. He slipped through the streets behind the shadow of Fatma Salam, his heart and his head full of the lightness of the kif.

When they got to the girl's house, Fatma Salam gestured to Mustapha to show him the way in, cautiously before vanishing. Mustapha entered the building. It was a small house of only two rooms. In the first room there was no one and Mustapha passed quickly through it to the door of the second room. He looked in and saw the girl asleep on a mat. Her face, unveiled in sleep, looked very beautiful to Mustapha. He went over to the mat and bent down to the girl and smelled the odor of her body in sleep. He grasped her shoulder and shook it. Her eyes opened immediately and she looked at Mustapha. "Don't make any noise," he said. But his head was full of kif, and he began to smile happily at the girl. "Wake up," he said, "the night is cool." Mustapha could feel a breeze stirring around the room. It reminded him of the wind on the beach, which had caused him to go into the cave. His thoughts seemed to be blowing past his head like the newspapers on the beach. If one of them hit you in the face, you could take it into the cave with you and read the news of the day. At the same time avoiding the heat of the sun! These thoughts began to run together, and all this time the girl was staring at Mustapha from her mat, like an angry bird. But was she angry? The night was cool. Finally the girl asked Mustapha what he wanted. "I saw you on the beach today," he said. "I know," said the girl, "you looked like you had no money." Mustapha said nothing, but took his mottoui out of his djellaba. There was a little bit of kif left in it. He emptied the last of the kif into his sebsi, lit it up and smoked it. The girl kept on staring at him, but his head was empty. The thoughts had stopped running through his head, which pleased him, and he knew what he was going to do. After a while he said, "My friend, Ali, told me to give this to his cousin Fatma

Salam. He said she would help me find you." Mustapha took the folded envelope out of his djellaba and handed it to the girl. She opened it up and took out ten dirhams. "There are ten dirhams in this envelope," said the girl. "I know," said Mustapha. The girl put the money back into the envelope, folded it up again, and slipped it under the mat. Mustapha put his mottoui and his sebsi on the floor next to the mat and then, with the kif still in his head, he lay down on the mat next to the girl.

The Last Gas Station

Carl Jordan had been a traveling salesman for 17 years. The gas shortages had made Carl into an anachronism. His job was obsolete. What profit was there in driving around the state—the whole state was Carl's territory—when it took you two to four hours of waiting in line back of the pumps to buy a few gallons of weak gasoline at a per-gallon price that destroyed any chance of coming out ahead on the day's sales? Better to stay home and collect unemployment, Carl's wife felt. But he was a man who loved the road, had the highway life in his blood and couldn't stand the idea of moping around the house waiting for the last rickety structures of the economy to collapse around him, as most of his neighbors were doing. Their jobs too had been snatched away by the fuel crisis of recent months, but they seemed less unhappy about it than Carl. They were paid by the government to stay at home, and that satisfied them—at least in the short term, for the paid layoff had very much the quality of an earned and long overdue holiday, one of which they'd been deprived throughout their working lives.

Carl stayed out on the road, even though his company no longer required it. In fact, his company was in the process of closing down; Carl found it harder and harder to replenish his sales stock after each selling trip, because the company was now selling out of surplus, and no longer produced new items. Sometimes he went out on the road with only half a load, or even, as time went by, no load at all. On those latter occasions he would rise in the morning, drive to his office on his few remaining drops of gas, and having found there was no stock on hand to pick up, quietly park at the tag end of the nearest gas line, waiting for his allotment.

By afternoon, he had gas. The sheer act of waiting left him dog tired. He drove to a bar, had a drink, and then drove out into the country, over empty roads. You had to get out of the city to see how dramatically the traffic flow was dwindling. No one drove for pleasure any more; Carl had the 6-lane expressway to himself, except for an occasional truck or police car.

60

In a way, it was pleasant to have nothing to sell. Instead of turning off at the suburban towns where he usually made his first stops, Carl kept on driving. The gas pedal felt good under his foot. Ahead, growing clearer in the flat, even light of mid-day, loomed the blue shapes of distant mountains. Shooting past off ramps and rest stops, Carl homed in on the mountains, and drove.

The sun beat down. Beads of sweat rolled down Carl's neck, wetting his shirt. The breeze created by his speedy passage blew in and dried it. Radio stations began to fade; Carl was getting out into vacant country. Low buttes ranged up parallel to the road. Hawks circled overhead in thermals. Sagebrush flopped against an ancient rusted propane tank, last remnant of a civilization whose detrital homesteads were now scattered more and more miles apart. Still Carl drove.

He had about a quarter of a tank of gas left by the time the sun started to go down. Now the mountains ahead were hulking up closer, shadowy purple with the sun going down brilliantly in yellows and blues behind them. Finally it flamed out fiery and red in its last rays and was gone. Carl kept on driving. He turned off the interstate highway onto a two-lane blacktop road. The blacktop quickly began to wind up into darkening foothills of juniper and scrub pine.

Carl had driven this road before. Once, fifteen years earlier, before their children were born, Carl and his wife had rented a summer cabin at a lake in these mountains. Carl had visited the area many times since. There was, he knew, a small resort community nestled in a canyon five or six miles up the blacktop road. The town had a gas station that stayed open at night to service truckers who were heading over the mountains. At least it had been open the last time Carl had been up this way. Now, he remembered as he drove, there were fewer trucks on the road. There was almost no diesel fuel available for any but the federally-subsidized interstate truck lines. The smaller in-state lines had gone out of business. Carl wondered if the station would be open after all. He peeked down at his gas gauge. The red needle wavered just above the bright green empty mark, occasionally bouncing against it.

Outside, it was completely dark now. There was no moon. Carl followed his headlights up the steep grade, around sharp corners where high walls of red rock loomed over the road, creating sudden sculptures in the path of Carl's brights. Around another corner, the road ahead, skimmed by the powerful beams, was enveloped in darkness where sheer cliffs dropped off into the blanketing night. Carl shivered. It was getting cold. He rolled up his window, then with one hand plucked a cigarette from the pack on the dashboard and lit it as he drove.

Carl's ears were popping; that was the altitude. He must be getting up high. He should be getting to the resort town about now— but the road was still winding up. The curves and grades got sharper and steeper, and—Carl had to admit to himself—less and less familiar. Could he have made a wrong turn? The thought made Carl nervous. He leaned forward tensely, squinting ahead into the small bath of light his beams made on the blacktop. Suddenly he felt a jolt. Something rattled against the bottom of the car. Peering out over the wheel, Carl saw that the blacktop road had turned into a rough dirt jeep trail. Rocks the size of a child's fist bounced against Carl's mudguards. He slowed down.

Carl didn't recognize this stretch of road at all. Maybe there was road construction going on; he'd been shunted off the blacktop into a detour without noticing it. But there had been no road markers or warning signs. Maybe this was simply work being done on the original road. But there was no indication of work going on. And, being honest with himself, Carl knew it was also not the original road. He was lost. The dirt track under him kept winding and climbing.

Well, there was no going back now; he'd just seen what lay behind him. Carl drove on over the rocky track at a few miles an hour, scanning the surrounding darkness for any familiar sign. Then, just as suddenly as it had ceased, the blacktop began again. Carl picked up speed. A moment later, his engine faltered. He forced the gas pedal down toward the floor. Nothing happened. Slowing involuntarily, he pulled over to the side of the road just as his motor died. The needle on the gas gauge had dropped to the left and clear of empty. Carl reached down and turned off the ignition.

He sat for a moment in the silence, thinking, and then got out of the car.

He heard crickets. There were trees along both sides of the road, and arching over it. They were big, dark deciduous trees. Carl figured he had to be at least ten thousand feet up by now. Trees like that couldn't grow at such an altitude. But there they were, a dark, enveloping presence on both sides of the road and over it.

Carl did not want to go into those trees. There they were. Well, he must have made a wrong turn. He knew there was nothing helpful behind him. He locked his car and started walking. The blacktop road quickly rounded a corner and plunged into absolute darkness. All Carl could make out were the vague shapes of huge, broad-leaved trees.

He walked for some time; possibly an hour, or two hours. It was hard to be sure. He was getting tired. Then he saw a light ahead. He started to run, but stumbled on his first step, twisting his ankle. He limped on. The light got closer. His ankle was hurting him badly now. His body wanted to stop and rest, but his mind told him this was no time to stop. He fell again. On all fours now, he crawled on.

The light ahead turned the trees a bright, glaring green. Carl looked up at them as he crawled. He couldn't see through their overarching branches. Behind the illuminated leaves there seemed to be great depths of darkness. Looking up, Carl did not notice an obstacle in the road. His knee came down on something rubbery. He drew back in horror, and cried out noiselessly, his mouth making a silent O. Coiled before him on the blacktop was an enormous King snake, glistening, black-spotted, bronzed, and apparently sound asleep. At least it was immobile, even after Carl's knee had landed on it. Reflexively, Carl's eyes sought the creature's head.

Its eyes were open and staring at him, but still the snake didn't move.

Horrified, Carl scrambled to his feet and staggered past the coiled beast. Ten feet down the road, he dropped to his knees again, hurting and exhausted. Now he crawled more tentatively, feeling-out the cold pavement ahead of him with his hands.

His hands and knees were bleeding, but Carl crawled on. The light ahead was quite bright now. It shone through the trees. Then the road turned and there was a clearing. Light filled it.

63

A gas station. Carl's eyes grew wide. Three old-fashioned red pumps, with bright white globes of light above them, advertising prices. A frame station house, bright yellow light flooding out of its windows. Above, a hanging sign, with lettering in Arabic.

At the pumps, a figure in overalls stood with its back to Carl. No, not overalls—some kind of robe? Carl's heart leaped in his chest. The station was open; the attendant was on duty. Carl wanted to call out, but he was too weak—no sound would come into his throat. He tried to scramble to his feet, fell, stood again, lurched forward. Now he was only five yards from the pumps.

The attendant still stood bent over the pumps. Wearing a robe with a hood, like a djellaba—an Arab robe. Carl's mind raced. Was he dreaming? Staggering, he rubbed bloody fists into his eyes. A few feet away, the hooded figure still stood, back to Carl, body bent over the pumps.

Carl had very little strength left. With it, he summoned two faint words.

"Excuse me," he said.

The hooded figure turned and with its back to the brightly lit pumps, faced Carl. Except that where its face should have been, there was only darkness.

Carl felt himself falling forward, into a slow free fall from which he woke up retired.

The Ten-Day Pitch

Joe Waters grew up in the red dirt and scrub pine farm country of North Georgia. As a boy the only notion Joe had about the outside world came from the drives he made with his father through the hills to towns like Dalton and Rome and Gainesville. Joe's dad, a dirt farmer who'd lost his land in the Depression, was now in the farm equipment business. Two or three times he took Joe along on business trips to Atlanta. Joe stood on Peachtree Street and wondered if the rest of the world out there could be as good as this. A cousin of the Waters family worked for Coca-Cola, and once when Joe was fourteen, he and his dad drove out to the man's office to visit. A tour of the plant was arranged for them. As Joe watched the sparkling green-tinted glass bottles roll along the machinery he couldn't help wandering in his mind.

Joe was a dreamy kind of boy in his way. Watching the Coke bottles go by, he daydreamed about the red lips and white teeth of smiling girls in towns thousands of miles away, beautiful girls smiling at their boyfriends as they tipped their heads back and swigged their Cokes. Joe had seen such girls in advertisements and also in the two or three dozen motion pictures he'd attended in Rome and Dalton and Gainesville, mostly with his friend Bob Bill Williams, a boy who could talk about women with the voice of experience. What you see in them pictures is just the box around the cake, Bob Bill said. The real thing, now that's even better. Bob Bill knew what he was talking about; he'd been to Memphis on his own. Joe watched the bright green bottles go by and thought of Bob Bill's stories and of the cool smiling white teeth and hot red lips of girls in Memphis and god knows where. It made his own teeth ache to think about that too much, because it was a thing Joe wanted bad. Any boy in his shoes would, he reckoned. Joe was not ashamed of these thoughts and daydreams he had. The only thing that brought him shame was his inability to make them into reality.

Daddy I need money

65

Give it to you honey
Daddy I need money now

Through the swinging doors of a wild place in Dalton where even his dad would never go, Joe had heard a smoky voice sing that song one hot summer evening a few years back, and the words had stayed in his mind like a funny kind of equation, a formula apart from experience which nonetheless could explain and maybe even determine it. What did they call it, an axiom? Joe watched the green bottles and felt his interior geometry of need do battle with his economic understanding. Tasting those white teeth and red lips was going to cost him money. That was the simple problem.

To Joe's North Georgia understanding, there was no way of trusting the democratic concept of equality of opportunity. Joe had watched his father's life too well and understood it too deeply to allow him to cherish any illusion about that. No, the only thing that made you equal was money.

*

Clyde Waters, Joe's father, had been raised on a turpentine mill in Northwest Georgia, and had himself worked as a mill hand until the closing of the company in the 1920s. Then he hired himself out for farm work until he had saved enough to buy his own small place, growning soybeans and tobacco. He'd married a girl from Milledgeville, and their first son was born in 1932, just when times were getting hard. He lost his farm in 1936, by which time there was also another son and a daughter to feed. In 1940 Joe came along, an event which shook the Waters family to its roots. Joe's mother, in fact, died of it, within a few months. This was no doubt a relief to her, but a hardship to the family. Joe's sister Evelyn, who was not quite eight when her mother died, took over the domestic management for the next seven years, until Clyde married again.

Clyde Waters had neither the capital nor the initiative to make much of a success out of his farm equipment business. He did, to his credit, manage a subsistence living out of it. His family never actually starved. By the time young Joe entered the local high school, his two older brothers had already left it, neither with a diploma, and gone away to the North to seek their fortunes—which meant in fact that they were looking for work somewhere in Kentucky or Tennessee. Evelyn had married and gone off to live in Birmingham with her husband, a steelworker. Joe and his dad and stepmother were all that remained of the family at home. Then, when Joe was in his second year of high school, Clyde Waters took sick and died.

*

Clyde Waters' second wife was a drinker. Clyde didn't leave her enough to support her, so she went on a long bender after his death, half out of resentment against him, and then left to live with a man in Waycross.

Joe had to quit school and go to work. He picked up a job as a clerk in a dry goods store in town—the manager had been a friend of his dad's. He got a $2 room in the local hotel, and wrote to tell his sister that he was fine. Evelyn had sent him a letter offering him a place in her home in Birmingham. His refusal now came as a relief to her, because she and her husband weren't getting along so well and certainly couldn't have afforded to support him, as Joe well knew.

"Got to make it on my own," Joe told himself. "Don't want to lean on nobody no more."

He didn't much care for the dry goods business, and was soon pumping gas in the filling station across the street. The man who owned the station was an expert mechanic; in six months he had taught Joe enough to enable the young man to work on almost any kind of car. One Saturday night Joe drove over to Athens with a friend and met a girl in a bar and went home with her. The girl did not have the smiling white teeth and hot red lips Joe had imagined in his daydreams, but she let him do it to her, and even better, her father ran an auto repair shop. The girl's father was so interested in getting his daughter married off that he hired Joe as a mechanic, even though Joe was only eighteen at the time. The man's daughter was twenty-two. The man reckoned Joe would quickly learn the trade and then enter the family. Joe had an innocent, trustworthy face, clear blue eyes and a pleasant, respectful manner. He paid his debts on time and went out of his way to be punctual and do all jobs well.

Joe got a room in a rooming-house in Athens and worked for the girl's father for a year. At the end of that time he left, claiming his mother was ill and that he had to go to New Orleans to be with her. Joe asked the girl's father for a letter of recommendation so that he could pick up temporary work in case he had to be in New Orleans for more than a few days. That was the last the girl or her father ever saw of him.

Joe did go to Louisiana, only the person he was visiting was not his poor departed mother, but his brother Frank, who was living in Lake Charles.

Frank was working in the feed and grain business. He gave Joe a job as a driver. Joe drove truck seven weeks for his brother, and then, using Frank's word and the Athens auto repairman's letter of recommendation, got another job driving and maintaining a small fleet of vehicles for a man who ran a charter transport company.

Lake Charles was good to Joe. He met a girl who reminded him of the girl in his Coca-Cola fantasy, and married her. He went to a local bank and took out a loan, with which he bought a small house.

The next year he ran into a man who was in the car importing business in Galveston. The man imported Volkswagens. He wanted a year off to go to Mexico for rest and recreation. He offered Joe twice the salary the charter transport job was paying. All Joe had to do was go to Galveston and run the car import business for a year. Joe accepted, leaving his bride and infant daughter behind in Lake Charles. "It's only for the time being," he said, kissing his wife goodbye.

The time being stretched into another year. The owner of the import business stayed in Mexico, happy to let Joe take care of the daily grind. Joe wrote to his wife explaining that conditions in Galveston weren't suitable for family living. He worked hard, made good money and paid off his Lake Charles loan. He took out a larger loan in Galveston and used the money to make a down payment on a gas station in Delray Beach, Florida.

His wife and daughter joined him in Florida. As usual, Joe quickly established relations with a local bank. He took out a substantial loan to finance extensive renovations on the gas station. The business was soon thriving, and Joe was able to pay off his Galveston note. But one day a man he knew came through town and offered him a piece of a used car agency in Alexandria, Virginia.

Joe had visited Alexandria and liked the area and the man's prospectus. He sold his gas station and moved to Alexandria with his wife and daughter and small son.

Over the next ten years Joe owned interests in businesses in a number of cities around the country. From Alexandria he moved to Atlanta, and from there to East St. Louis, Ill., and from there to Phoenix, and from there to Missoula, Montana, and from there to Aspen, Colorado, where at the age of 34 he found himself with a net worth of some $35,000, a whistle-clean financial profile at nine respectable banks around the country from which he'd borrowed money over the years, a $105,000 home he was still paying for, a wife he didn't like, two kids heading for college, and sufficient living expenses to prevent him, in his view, from ever graduating out of the rat race he'd been caught in for years.

Joe was tired of it all. He'd paid off all his debts on time, strived and hustled to make himself a financial success, but still he wasn't clear of the workaday cycle. Joe wanted, more than anything else, to be free and clear of it.

The daydream image that had survived from Joe's childhood— bright rows of green Coca-Cola bottles and the smiling white teeth and hot red lips of women enjoying them—was for him a symbol of the ease and glamor that his actual experience had never contained. It was an image that represented all the good experiences that were perpetually out of his reach. The time-honored Horatio Alger formula—that honest application and hard work lead to success, fulfillment and satisfaction—hadn't worked for him. After all his schemes and hustles, Joe still had not attained the plateau of ease he had always desired. He was not yet a rich man, and at the present rate he was never going to be one.

Joe began to spend more and more of his free time thinking about possible avenues of escape. He grew more and more abstracted;

when spoken to, he sometimes did not reply. He sat at his desk at the office or at home in front of the television and let his mind wander.

A man he'd met at a business luncheon had told Joe about a place called Moorea, in Tahiti, where if you married a native there were no taxes, and where beautiful Polynesian girls walked around with—in the man's words—"their hair down to their butts and nothing inside their heads but making you happy."

That sounded good to Joe.

*

Like the pedals of a treadmill, the daily motions of Joe's business life had become an unconscious path he followed by rote. "I've always worked my ass off," he told himself. "Where has it got me?"

Joe knew he was hooked into the economic Main Line. Every day he went out to make another dime and came home with a lot of pain and worrying he didn't need. It had been that way for years and now things were only gettting worse. "Another day, another dollar," had once been Joe's motto. Now a dollar was only a half dollar, or worse. It didn't make sense to him.

Joe had been in business in America too long. Times were changing. Hard work was no longer enough. Bread cost a dollar a loaf. It made Joe want to laugh, when it didn't make him feel like crying.

Joe wanted out. But he wanted out *legally*. His mind searched for a way. He stopped recognizing his friends on the street, forgot his children's names, avoided a local girl he'd been having a half-hearted affair with, and spent all his time brooding about what to do. He wanted to fix things up so that he would never have to do another day's work. The question of how to do that without going to jail haunted his nights and days.

Joe wanted to find that tiny hole in the wall, that pinpoint he could squeeze through and glide on all the way into Easy Street.

*

At present Joe ran a truck rental business in Aspen. He had established good relations with a local bank. He had a fifteen year track record of total financial reliability, had never been late in paying off a debt. The banks he dealt with knew this, and appreciated it. Joe had such a smooth business style, so much charm and natural courtesy in his manner that he couldn't help winning over anybody he did business with. This went double for bankers, who were suckers for Joe's sweet business pitch.

One day as Joe sat in his office staring vacantly at a stack of unpaid bills on his desk, an idea went through his head with the speed and suddenness of a shot.

He had been thinking about his banks—counting in his mind the banks he'd done business with. There were nine of them. The figure spun in his mind. Nine. Ninepins. Idly, Joe thought of a juggler twirling ninepins. What if each pin were a bank?

Juggling ninepins. Juggling nine banks.

Joe reached for the phone, intending to call his lawyer, then stopped. He could share this with no one, not even his lawyer.

He got out his pocket calculator and ran through some figures. For an hour he worked feverishly with calculator, pencil and paper. Finished, he lit a cigarette, then picked up the telephone and called a local travel agency.

*

Each of Joe's nine banks still kept in touch with him, and vice versa. He had been careful not to terminate his accounts, leaving small deposits of a few hundred dollars in each bank in case there was ever the need to write local checks in those towns. Fastidious in all his money dealings, he had also as a matter of policy sent current financial statements to each bank every year. Although Joe's liquid assets never went above the $30,000–$50,000 range, he had considerable property on paper, and was always able to emphasize this effectively in his financial statements.

These statements and his credit history built up for Joe an essential credibility that made his banks consider him a model customer.

Joe wanted to stay inside the law.

He knew a man can't be convicted for owing money in America.

On this particular afternoon, he sat late in his office, thinking things over and over.

Rows of Coca-Cola bottles, green and clear and sparkling, poured down an endless assembly line in his mind, like a personal vision of heaven.

At seven o'clock Joe left the office, went home, and locked himself up in his study with a pot of coffee and all his financial records.

He had to prepare his pitch.

*

Sometime after midnight Joe called the girl he'd been having an affair with and asked her to meet him at a local bar. Puzzled by his sudden interest—he hadn't called in weeks—she immediately agreed. When she met him and found out what he wanted, she was disagreeably surprised.

"You're leaving the country and you want to use *me* for a contact after you're gone?"

"Why not you? I've thought about it. You're the only person I know I can trust."

"Oh yeah?" The girl laughed in Joe's face. "You better think about it some more."

Despite the girl's unpleasant tone, Joe smiled his most appealing smile and squeezed her hand.

"Don't be so hard," he said ingenuously.

The girl's eyes were on Joe like steel on granite. "What's in it for me?"

"I'll take care of you," Joe said. "Whatever you do for me, you'll be paid for."

"That's more like it," the girl said. She sipped her beer. "Where you going, anyway?"

"I can't tell you until it's set up," Joe said.

The girl turned ironic. "Not so happy at home after all?"

"It's got nothing to do with her."

The girl nodded knowingly, disbelieving him.

"Got to be up early," Joe said, glancing at his watch. "I'll drive you home."

72

The next day was Sunday. Joe told his wife he would be gone for several days, maybe a week. An emergency business trip, he explained. He called and left word at the office that he would be out of town on a personal matter, and then drove into Denver. From Stapleton he caught a plane to Washington, D.C. At Dulles he rented a car and drove to Alexandria, where first thing Monday morning he laid his pitch on the line.

At 9:00 a.m. Joe walked from the motel to his bank, went to the desk of the loan officer, greeted the man (who remembered his first name) with a warm, personable smile and powerful handshake, and then sat down to talk. He wanted to apply for a $50,000 one year note, Joe told the officer. The officer smiled politely and listened. Joe went on talking. He wanted the note for personal reasons, he said. He wanted that fact specified on the note. This was not unique; Joe had taken out such a note on this bank before. The officer nodded. "You have my current financial statement on record," Joe said. The officer nodded again.

"I think we'd want you to prepare a new statement," he said gently.

Joe shook his head. "Take too much time," he said. He edged forward in his chair, as if about to get up.

"Well," the officer said tentatively, "I suppose your present statement could be updated?"

"Don't *need* to update it," Joe said. He had to be careful here. There were two major hazards he had to avoid. The note had to be for an unspecified purpose, *and* he had to make sure not to sign a new statement. He couldn't make the new statement out honestly, because to do so he'd have to include the fact that he was borrowing money elsewhere concurrently with the present loan. To conceal this fact would be a crime. Paramount in Joe's plan was his desire to avoid criminal liability. To make some simple mistake he might later be extradited for would make all his best efforts a waste of time, he knew.

"Don't need to?" the officer repeated.

"No sir," Joe said emphatically. "No changes in my situation at all."

73

The loan officer's cool grey eyes crossed with Joe's cold blue ones for a moment so fleeting you wouldn't have noticed if you'd been standing next to them. Then the officer pushed a button on his desk and spoke through an intercom system, requesting Mr. Waters' financial statement.

He then handed Joe a loan application form and a pen with the name of the bank stamped on it. Joe took the pen, carefully perused the legend on its side—the inscribed lettering was gold on a blue field, like sunlight on the ocean—and while many unrelated thoughts rushed through his head in a confusing swirl that made him feel like he was swooning, he bent the pen toward the fresh white paper and began to sketch out the blueprint of his future.

*

Later that morning Joe drove back to Washington. He headed straight for National Airport, where he deposited his rented car and caught the lunch hour plant to Atlanta. That afternoon he performed in the office of the loan executive at his Atlanta bank, one of the biggest and most prestigious in Georgia. He left before closing time with positive assurances about his chances of obtaining a $50,000 one year note. The note would be for unspecified personal use and would be issued without the preparation of a new financial statement by the borrower, Joseph Waters.

*

People make the mistake of thinking banks are superhuman, that they are perfect—like big perfect computer chips floating in the sky.

Banks are human. They are managed by human beings, and therefore they make mistakes. For that bank in Atlanta, Joe Waters was such a mistake, just as he'd been a mistake for the bank in Alexandria, and just as, in the next few days, he would become a mistake for seven other banks in the southern and western United States.

But even afterward, when their mistakes had been discovered,

74

not one of those banks would have said that Joe Waters was anything but a pleasure to do business with.

*

Monday night, Joe flew from Atlanta to Miami. On Tuesday morning he was waiting outside his bank in Delray Beach when it opened. That same afternoon he flew to New Orleans, rented a car, and drove to Lake Charles. On Wednesday morning he made his pitch successfully at the bank in Lake Charles, and then drove on to Galveston. Blowing down the highway along the Gulf at 80, he made it to his bank an hour before closing, in plenty of time to get his business done.

His pitches got shorter, faster and sweeter with practice. The one in Galveston took him only 25 minutes, from handshake to signature.

*

Joe drove into Houston very early Thursday morning, early enough to catch a plane that put him in St. Louis in time to rent another car and drive across the river to East St. Louis before his bank opened there. He was the day's first customer.

At 3:15 that afternoon, he was in Phoenix.

On Friday morning he was in Missoula, Montana. There was a heavy thunderstorm in Missoula that afternoon, but Joe hardly noticed it. He was inside a bank.

He flew into Denver Friday night and made his final pitch in Aspen on Saturday morning.

Everything went like clockwork. Even weakened by fatigue, Joe's pitch was flawless. The Aspen bank fell in line with the others, like the last domino in a chain.

Joe was home in time to watch the opening game of the college football season on television Saturday afternoon. Exhausted, he had no idea which teams were playing, and fell asleep in his chair midway through the second quarter. His wife was unable to awaken him until several hours after dark, at which time he got up, shaved and showered, and went out to look for a long slow drink.

*

Joe was back in his truck rental agency office bright and early on Monday morning. He put all his calls on hold, stuffed all his mail and memos into an unused file cabinet, canceled all his appointments for the day and had a pot of black coffee brought in.

Then he chased his secretary out of the office and reached for the phone.

It took Joe all that day, and the one after that, and the one after that, to make all the telephone calls he had to make.

By Wednesday evening he had secured all his deals.

On Thursday the cash began to arrive. By the following Monday, all the money was in: Joe had $450,000. His airline tickets and reservations were waiting for him in Denver.

*

On the plane to Papeete, Joe had plenty of time to calculate. He planned to invest his money in 12% certificates, which would earn him an annual $54,000 in interest, free of taxes if he could find a suitable Polynesian wife in the next 12 months . . . and from the appearance of the Tahitian-native stewardess on the Air Asia 747, that would be no problem.

He made a note in his head to wire money to the girl in Aspen every month, for anonymous delivery to his family. He didn't want to leave too bad an impression with the folks back home.

After a while he put his note pad and calculator away and tipped back in his reclining seat. Out the window the cloud armadas stretched away into a blue-gold distance where, if he half-closed his eyes and squinted into it, Joe could see not only the gilded beauty of the Pacific sunset but the warm red lips and bright white teeth of a million smiling, relaxed girls, drinking Coca-Colas and willing to make him happy for the rest of his days.

Success Story

Dennis Ackroyd is a somewhat crazed loner-type Vietnam veteran, with a dishonorable discharge, a broken marriage and a trail of missed opportunities in his background. Unknown to anyone, he writes a wild obscure novel about his experience of post-Vietnam America and sends it to a N.Y. publisher under the name "Carla Speer" (his dead Vietnam buddy once knew a girl by that name) c/o a P.O. Box in Boulder.

The publisher puts off reading it for months, due to the state of the MS., but finally does so, and totally loves the novel. Only catch is, he has lost the author's return envelope. He remembers only that the return address is a P.O. Box in Boulder. The MS. is signed simply "Carla Speer." So he writes a letter addressed to

> Carla Speer
> Writer of fiction
> P.O. Box ?
> Boulder, Colo.

In Boulder there's a woman named Carol Steen, who writes short stories for magazines on a free lance basis. One day she opens up her post office box and finds the letter from the publisher addressed to "Carla Speer."

The letter informs Carla Speer that while he feels it is uneven and incomplete, her manuscript is of great interest to the publisher, and that he would like to know something more about her and her background "as a prelude to our working together on your book."

Carol Steen has been working on a novel for years. She has shopped chapters around to publishers, without success. She has also flooded the mails with short story submissions to magazine editors, several of which have been accepted. Consequently the postal officials are quite used to placing large and small packages from New York publishing companies in Carol's post office box. It's evidently the result of a natural error that one of these officials placed the letter from the publisher to Carla Speer into Carol's box.

Carol takes the letter out of the box, opens it, reads it quickly, stuffs it into her purse, and leaves the post office. She gets into a white VW, parked outside, and drives off.

Dennis Ackroyd stomps around his rented room in Boulder with a fixed look on his face. Occasionally he cackles hideously. He seems seriously crazed. On one wall of the furnished room there is a large American flag. Every once in a while Dennis interrupts his march around the room to stop and salute the flag.

At home, Carol Steen stuffs the letter into a pile of unanswered mail and goes to work. She makes coffee, lights a cigarette, sits down at her typewriter and rolls in a fresh sheet of paper. Behind horn rim glasses, her brows furrow in thought. She begins typing.

Ackroyd paces manically up and down in his room. There's a knock on the door. He stops pacing, his shoulders droop, he shrinks back into a reasonably normal-looking person. Says, "Come in!" It's a woman in her late 20s, in jeans and sweater, with long black hair and a hollow-eyed, blank-looking face bespeaking drug addiction. It is Dennis's wife. They haven't seen each other for six months. She asks Dennis for 50 dollars. He refuses, claiming he doesn't have the money. She leaves, angry. Dennis goes to his dresser and takes out a ragged manila envelope stuffed with greenbacks. He takes out the bills, tears them into little pieces and flushes them down the toilet.

Carol Steen sits at her typewriter, smoking, her head leaning on one hand which is propped up by her elbow. She stares at the words on the page in front of her, moans softly, and gets up from the typewriter. She goes to her refrigerator and takes out a can of beer. She pours a glass of beer, sits down at the kitchen table and drinks it, smoking and thinking. The beer finished, she gets up, goes back into her study, digs out the publisher's letter and re-reads it. Then she sits down, rolls a fresh sheet of paper into her typewriter and begins typing again. Over her shoulder, we see that she is addressing the publisher in New York. In her letter, she thanks the publisher for his interest, asks to hear his terms, and requests that he send her a xerox copy of her manuscript; she will need a copy for revision, she explains. She signs her letter "Carla Speer," but in a postscript informs the publisher that her real name is Carol Steen and that henceforth he should address all communications to her home address in Boulder. "I believe I may be dispensing with my pseudonym soon," she concludes the postscript.

A week later, Carol receives a copy of the "Carla Speer" MS. from New York by first-class air express. She reads it, shaken by its force. She sees it is very imperfect as a piece of writing, but she also recognizes it as the product of an inspired, visionary mind. She writes to the publisher, suggesting revisions. He writes back, confirming her ideas and proposing new ones of his own. With the publisher's intelligent help, Carol shapes Ackroyd's work into an excellent book, which is to be published under her name. She receives $10,000 from the publisher. Two months later—and with the publication still six months away—the book is sold to a Hollywood movie company. Carol receives $450,000. She moves to the Bahamas.

In Boulder, Dennis Ackroyd goes to see a movie that's been recommended to him by his landlord. The title is unfamiliar, the title of a best-selling recent book, but the events of the film and much of the dialogue are shockingly familiar. His mind reeling, Dennis leaves the film. He walks to a bookstore, goes in, finds a copy of the book, and begins leafing through it. His eyes grow wild. He throws the book down, runs out into the street.

The next morning, Dennis phones the publisher in New York and charges that the Carol Steen bestseller is actually his own work. It takes him several minutes to get the publisher on the phone.

"That's my work, you bastard."

"Who's this?"

"Dennis Ackroyd. That Carol Steen book, I wrote it. Don't you remember? I sent it to you under a fake name, Carla Speer."

"Who you trying to kid, buddy? Every jerk on the street knows that used to be Carol's writing name."

"Huh?"

"Sorry, pal. The trick's been tried before. If you got a plagiarism claim, get in touch with our lawyers."

The phone clicks dead.

Dennis has no way to prove authorship unless he can prove he "is" Carla Speer.

He has to find the real Carla Speer.

His dead buddy was from Chicago. Dennis flies there to look for Carla. His dead buddy's family and friends never heard of her. Dennis's buddy never cared much for girls, they say. At least not to talk about them. One guy Dennis talks to, though, a guy who owns a gas station where Dennis's buddy worked, says Dennis's buddy had a girl from Kentucky. Dennis's dead buddy met her in a bar. They spent a night together, the gas station guy says. Dennis's buddy talked about her a couple of times later, at work. All the gas station guy knows is that she was from Kentucky. It's the only girl he ever heard Dennis's buddy talk about. What her name was, he can't recall. Dennis's buddy went directly from that gas station job to Vietnam.

Dennis takes a bus to Kentucky. He rides around Louisville by buses and taxis, looking out the window. He hitchhikes into the country and spends two weeks beating the bushes around Kentucky, reading phone books and asking questions in bars, but he doesn't find Carla Speer. Finally he is arrested in a bar fight, after asking one too many questions, and is jailed for vagrancy. The story makes the local newspaper. A cop tells the court reporter about how this nut claims he's looking for a girl who can help him prove he wrote a book that's worth a half a million dollars. The reporter writes it up as an amusing human interest item. It makes the wire services. Carol Steen, who is visiting Hollywood to work as a paid consultant to the team of scenariasts who are turning her second novel into a movie, notices the item in the *L.A. Times*. She shows it to her business agent, who's accompanying her on the trip.

He laughs nervously.

"Obviously a lunatic," he says.

They are drinking in an expensive bar in Hollywood. Her agent coughs. Carol doesn't seem to have heard him; she hasn't replied.

"Obviously the guy's some kind of nut," he repeats.

She sips her apéritif.

"Relax, Charlie," she says. "We've got nothing to worry about."

"What's that mean?" The agent pulls hard at his bourbon.

"I talked to Dennis Ackroyd on the phone this morning."

"To who?"

"Ackroyd, the man who is in jail in Kentucky."

"You *spoke* to him?"

"I called the jail. They let me talk to him."

"Why'd you do *that?*"

"Wouldn't *you* be interested in talking to the man who wrote the book that made you rich and famous?"

The agent is perspiring heavily, despite the air conditioning.

"Quit kidding around, baby. It ain't funny." He peers around the room. "Somebody might be listening, you know?"

"I'm sorry, darling. I couldn't help pulling your leg. You looked so worried."

Relief floods the agent's face. He tugs long and hard at his drink, draining it; signals across the room with his face and fingers for a refill.

"All right, I get upset. But it's a world full of foul balls, baby. In our business you run into them ever day. Wait till you been out here a while, you'll understand."

Carol smiles and stares over the tall glasses at a point in space two inches above her agent's face.

"I've got to run," she says. "They're waiting at the studio."

"I'll drive you there," the agent says.

"That's all right. They're sending a car. It's probably outside right now."

"Marvelous," says the agent, fresh respect showing in his voice.

Dennis staggers down the street in Boulder. It is winter; snow falls, covering him. The pavement is icy. Dennis slips on the ice and falls. As the camera gets closer, we see his snow-coated raiment is actually the tattered American flag which once hung on the wall of his room. Now Dennis has no room, it appears. He wears his flag on his back, like a squaw's wrap. He is down on all fours, shaking his head. Now he gets up. Some snow falls off him, but not all of it. He shuffles down the street, still shaking his head.

The San Diego Report

Feb. 11 (Bolinas): (6 a.m.) it's still dark when I wake up, shave, put on brown suit & Mike Goldberg Italian wedding shirt, pack poems in an envelope, pack acid tab inside antibiotic capsule, kiss the girls goodbye, run out the door & jump in Jack's bus, say hi to Ebbe, Joanne & Jack. We drive to the airport, get there at 9. I go to the PSA desk & buy a round trip ticket to San Diego. Ebbe buys same for Joanne, I board PSA Flight 2:30 for San Diego nonstop, leaving at 9:30. The plane takes off. I tell Joanne I've always wanted to fuck while taking off. Joanne takes out the Esterol spansule Lewis gave her, pours some of the time pellets into her palm & swallows them, I do the same, but look to see if the stewardess is watching. She isn't. She's wearing an orange cap, suit and bloomers. Her black hair is tied up in a bun under her cap. I tell Joanne she'd look better with her hair down. (The stewardess). Joanne tells me she saw two stewardesses lacquering themselves in the airport ladies' room. Lacquering their hair. The 727 is buzzing above the clouds. Pure blue air goes by slowly and billowy polar landscapes pass. I read that Elvin Hayes has called his teammates losers. I look up the entertainment page of the San Diego paper and start to pore over the movie ads but can't pay attention, so I borrow Joanne's notebook and write a work called "Giovanna in San Diego" while she looks through her poems and pretty soon the plane lands in San Diego. Two students at UCSD, Kathy Acker and her boyfriend Lenny Newfield, are waiting for us. They have a car (borrowed) so we jump in and drive out to David Antin's house in Solano Beach, some 25 miles by freeway. Lennie driving while Kathy bad-mouths the local scene by way of putting us in the know but Joanne and I look out the window and spot a tiny mesa which reminds us of Bolinas and we all talk some more and finally get to David's house, a green stucco bungalow on the edge of a cliff over the ocean, where we're kindly greeted and served lunch and beer and more talk, this time more interesting, with

David and his wife Eleanor—they've just returned from New York where Eleanor had a show at Gain Ground Gallery—their son Blaise Cendrars (2½) charges around behind toy jet airplanes and throws napkins at me while we eat avocados and anchovies & discuss nakedness. It occurs to me the question is more real here where it's warm than in Bolinas where you'd freeze your ass off if it wasn't covered. It occurs to me that Eleanor will—uh, would—look great without clothes. Everybody drinks more beer and laughs. I go in the bathroom and drop the antibiotic/acid cap, then to the patio where I fall into a chaise lounge in the sun to read the proofs of John Ashbery's *The Double Dream of Spring*, which David A. is reviewing for the Nation, but the chaise lounge is broken and I fall straight through and out of it onto the ground, horribly scraping my inside right forearm on jagged metal from nowhere. I go in and Eleanor gives me the Phisohex and I wash the cut and go back outside and lie down, this time on the grass, in the sun, which is very hot, under the very blue sky. Minutes/hours later everybody else comes outside too. Lennie and Kathy want to talk about poetry. Joanne talks about rock lyrics. Lennie and Kathy hate rock lyrics, but love Jackson Mac Low. David and I talk about James Dickey, then Robert Bly—then Blaise Cendrars, who's in David's lap as he is talking, suddenly grins and takes a huge runny shit. David goes inside to change his shirt. Joanne goes inside to look over her poems. Finally Lennie and Kathy and Joanne and I leave for the reading in "our" car. David and Eleanor will come later. We get to the UCSD campus and spend an hour or so checking out the landscape, looking for postcards, and smoking cigarettes while lots of students walk by and look at us blankly—Joanne and I are sitting on a bench, waiting for Kathy and Lennie to gopher our checks. They show up and say the checks won't be ready until tomorrow. We say that's OK. Then a bearded prof type named Ben Van Wright shows up, introduces himself as editor of the *Lemming Review* and starts a rap about Richard Brautigan which leads into soliciting poems for the *Lemming Review*. Then it's time to go to the reading—which is held in a peaceful anonymous spacey afternoon room and attended by about twenty-five people.

We read two sets each and it's a good reading. Quickly afterwards everyone splits—David and Eleanor go to teach evening classes, while we walk to the car with Kathy and Lennie and someone named Larry, who it turns out owns the car, and someone else (nameless) who tells us about how to measure the height of a building with a barometer. We all pile in, Larry drives, it's getting dark and the ocean sky is orange and polluted and lavender and beautiful and it's hot, like St. Louis in June, and we drive through the night. In La Jolla we stop and Nameless Barometer gets out. Then we stop at Food Basket. Lennie and Kathy and Joanne go in to buy some chow. I stay in the car and rap with Larry, who's in his fifth year of college-to-avoid-the-draft, about "how to get out of it." Then we discuss California, which we both like—he's spent his whole life here in San Diego—et cetera—they come back with the groceries and we start off again, this time to get what Kathy and Lennie call "the stuff." First we go by Melvin's place, Lennie runs in, but Melvin ain't home—no stuff. So we motor through a few more neon editions of La Jolla, Del Mar, Mission Beach or wherever and stop in an alley, Lennie makes the run and this times comes out with de stuff—zoom back across fifty avenues and finally come to Kathy and Lennie's pad on B Street. Out, up and in. Kathy goes to the kitchen to dress the roast. I put on a record of Satie orchestral music. Larry sinks into a chair. Joanne examines some of the millions of books that are propped on homemade bookshelves all around the apartment—which is big, lots of back rooms, walk around, drink wine, Lennie slowly rolls the stuff, no papers—Lennie likes to dump the tobacco out of a Salem and replace it with the stuff. Although this operation could be simply performed by one, Lennie asks Joanne to help by tapping the stuff with a pencil so it'll slide gradually from a piece of paper held by Lennie into the empty Salem tube. All this takes infinite years. Finally three joints of stuff have been rolled. We light up and pass them around. It's fantastic grass. Instantly we're all stoned. Who's here? Lennie has long blond hair. He picks up a stuff-filled Salem and wiggles it back and forth in front of Joanne's face, then asks what does that remind you of? It reminds everyone of a limp prick. Joanne refuses to answer. I say "a turtle." More stuff comes around. Larry is sinking deeper and deeper and deeper in his chair. His face takes on an expression of ageless mirth. Kathy runs back and forth between the roast and the stuff. She is wearing a mini-skirt that can't be longer than—you can see her ass, about two inches of it, below the bottom edge of the skirt. She has lots of poetry books. She attended Brandeis for two years and is married. Lennie is married too. He edited a magazine called *Omphalos* once. He is twenty-seven. He is nodding out. He is in bliss. Kathy is talking. She loved Rilke until she came to hate all Christians. I vanish into the back room with a parcel of stuff. The back room is tiny and lit by a triad of bulbs—red, blue, yellow. Beyond the back room is another room where an old man lies dying. Occasionally he coughs. The sound seems to be amplified, rather than diminished, by the distance (a few feet) through the wall. I very quietly search for some papers. I find some dressmakers' patterns and scissors (Kathy uses this room for sewing and also as a stash for poetry books) and cut the pattern-paper into papers for rolling stuff. The first few test joints don't burn too well, so I look around some more and find (bathroom) some Tampax—Eureka! Tampax comes packed in a soft white paper of perfect consistency for rolling. Roll and smoke several joints of stuff in Tampax papers. Open the window. Nighttime red light roominghouse night in midwest summers I've never known about suddenly is realized as James M. Cain Southern California vision—a million carlights twinkle and move in the warm night out the window—all over San Diego. I'm lying on the bed. Years later I pick a few poetry books off the shelf and strum through them for 1 second. Joanne comes in. She goes out. I go too. We're all in front again. Lennie is dead. Larry is dead. Kathy is still alive—still fixing dinner? Joanne is social and graceful and brings the dead back to life and moves on easy lights, lightly easing everyone over to the beef. We pack away lots of beef without even knowing it. Then Turkish coffee. Ben Van Wright shows up, to read some manuscripts to us. The poems aren't his, they're by somebody named Arthur Lane. They're hideous. He is creepy. He gets creepier to us as we smoke a million more stuff. I fade into the back room again, years later Ben leaves. Before he leaves he tells me he is Philbert Fuckknuckles. I'm not sure what he means. I'm in the back room. The old man coughs. The poetry books are asleep. The night is white. It is morning. Kathy and Lennie wake up. We all have breakfast and decide to miss the bus to the airport in order to have time for some more stuff—finally call a cab, it comes, goes away again, comic seconds, more cab comes, we get in, drive away to airport, get on plane, fly to San Francisco. The plane nearly crashes into, instead of landing on the runway, but my heart is full of Escatrol or whatever it's called and only misses about ½ a beat, and at the last second the pilot flips down his rudder, straightens out, lands, & later we're home.

The Last Stop

Getting to the airport on time was always half the battle. Picking up the check was the other half. Automatically the poet's hand dived into the inside pocket of his down vest. Paper crinkled there—last night's payment. So far so good. The trip was going well. The poet listened inside himself: he was tired, yes, that was natural (he had just done five readings in four days) but all his systems were still functioning. Biology and poetry were not at odds— that was a principal tenet of the poet's life. Now even the hum of the plane's engines seemed reassuring, part of a perfect guiding order that guaranteed the rightness of the universe.

He had been chauffeured to the airport—in an eighty-mile-an-hour whirlwind of a drive—by two female graduate students with whom he may well have spent the night after his reading of the previous evening. It was hard to remember that evening in much detail. On the day after a reading, faces and events always tended to flow together in the poet's mind, mixing with the faces and events from other evenings, other parties. Tours always produced a crazy blur of experience in his memory. But that was all right. The poet was not into memory much.

The sun was shining, it was a crisp, clear blue day, and the short flight over the mountains was a pleasure. The poet sat next to a traveling salesman who spent the whole trip working out with a pocket calculator and a ledger pad. This was a relief; there was nothing the poet liked less than having a garrulous seat-mate on the way to a reading—unless, of course, the seat-mate was attractive and female. Even then, the poet preferred her not to be too talkative. Flying to a new town, you had to gather up the loose parts of your personality scattered by the night before, and concentrate them. There was a certain ritual to preparing for a reading. These final quiet moments of airborne self-communion had their purpose. Carefully stored up now, later they would unfurl into a sail of interior calm that would carry the poet effortlessly through his next reading.

He rested his briefcase on his drink-tray and sorted through sheaves of poems, putting them in order, making a correction or revision here and there, wherever his eye fell on an offending passage. The poet believed in a flow of creative activity that never stopped. It was always compelling him to modify his poems, so that years after their publication they often assumed new forms unfamiliar even to listeners who knew all his stuff by heart. They attended his readings to hear the work they had so long admired in print, and came away amazed at how different it sounded aloud. The difference between what they expected and what they heard was due to these small revisions the poet was constantly making, preventing any of his poems from ever achieving an absolute final form. This way, the poet felt he was eluding definition, solidification, predictability—things that represented to him everything unpleasant in life. Not to mention death itself, an experience he always associated in his mind with publication.

The poet pondered all this as he peered down at the peaks that glittered in the late afternoon sun under a diamond mantle of snow. Musing, revising, his inner spring began to coil tight, giving him the tension he needed to do justice to his poems.

The plane dipped and began its slow descent into the intermontane valley where the College of the Rockies had its campus. A private school with a steep tuition scale, CR was well known for its blue chip cultural program, which included regular visits to the campus by artists and writers of every type. Two or three times a year, the English Department flew a big name poet in to read. Creeley had been here last fall, the poet knew, and Brautigan had come in the spring before that. Four months earlier he himself had received a letter offering him $500 plus expenses to read his poems at CR. He accepted, and specified a date that would allow him to conjoin this reading with five others into a lucrative chain—six readings in five days for $2500, a standard tour.

A small bearded man in a topcoat was waiting for the poet at the gate as he came off the plane. This was David Fussfaster, a minor poet who worked in the English Department at CR and was a member of the Visitors' Committee, the departmental body which had invited the poet to read. The poet had never laid eyes on Fussfaster, and vice versa. But the poet's face was famous. As he came through the gate, the bearded man in the topcoat thrust one gloved hand out like a ramrod, surprising the poet considerably. The plane ride had made him tenser than he knew, and now he jumped back, startled.

"Welcome. I'm Fussfaster."

"Swell," said the poet, remembering where he was and relaxing. He shook Fussfaster's hand and gave the smaller man his traveling bag to carry. Fussfaster took it and stood there, seemingly paralyzed. On his face was a fixed, hysterical grin.

"Welcome!"

"Which way?" said the poet.

"Oh. Over here."

Deferential as a valet, Fussfaster pointed the way down a long corridor, then let the poet take the lead.

Fussfaster's car was parked in the airport lot. It was new and sleek. Fussfaster drove slowly and asked many questions. Obviously nervous, he didn't notice the poet was paying no attention to him at all. The poet's replies to his literary queries were polite, noncommittal, largely monosyllabic, and automatic. This was a conversation he had had a thousand times before and could conduct in his sleep. He gazed out his side window at a snow-decked alpine valleyscape.

They were driving through a long, broad meadow. On both sides rocky ledges sprang up sharply, occasional condominiums sprouting from their faces like coarse wooden flowers. Soon the jerry-built outskirts of the college town pitched into view from the top of a small rise.

"That's the college," Fussfaster said, pointing out a cluster of stone and red brick buildings two or three miles across the valley.

"Ah," said the poet.

"We'll go to my place first and have dinner," Fussfaster said. "The reading isn't till eight." He glanced at the poet. "That all right with you?"

"Sure," said the poet. "Can we get a drink at your place?"

"Of course. Or we can stop for one. Whichever you please."

"Let's stop, if we've got time," the poet said.

Fussfaster made a couple of turns and they were in the town's business district. He parked in front of a place with potted plants in the window. They went inside and while Fussfaster drank beer and asked many questions, the poet tossed down a rapid series of double screwdrivers and assessed the waitress situation with a scrutiny that had been refined by long experience.

Between his second and third beers Fussfaster passed from the interrogative phase into its logical successor, the phase of bitching and moaning. Having exhausted for the moment his curiosity about the outside world, he now lapsed back into complaining about the world immediately at hand. The poet had never yet been to a college where the department types didn't complain at length about their jobs and surroundings.

"It's a dumb wasteland," Fussfaster was saying. "Nothing but playboys, jocks and rednecks. Nobody knows anything. Nobody appreciates anything. You think these people care about Gary Snyder?" He shook his head.

"Hmm," the poet said, staring blankly across the room at a blonde, pony-tailed waitress. Leaving his eyes to wander, his mouth smiled sympathetically at Fussfaster, an automatic smile.

"I envy you," the bearded man was saying. "Christ, don't I? I envy you your freedom, above all. Freedom to write. Oh, I could always quit. But it's such a damn easy thing, this teaching—you can just go on and on with it. Of course, it eats up *all* your time."

"They pay you for it, don't they?" the poet said absently.

"That's just it," Fussfaster said. "There's my wife and kid to consider. Who's going to feed them if I quit to write poems?"

"You got me," the poet said. The blonde waitress had gone back into the kitchen. He looked Fussfaster in the eye. Fussfaster was still bitching and moaning. The poet tuned him out and ordered another double screwdriver from the waitress nearest to hand. She was tall, slim, with long black hair that trailed halfway down her back. The poet was just considering asking her what time she got off work when Fussfaster glanced at his watch, and suddenly clapped a palm to his forehead.

"Quarter past seven," he said. "God. Clare will be furious."

"Clare?" the poet asked.

"My wife. She's serving dinner at seven."

"Was, you mean."

Fussfaster winced. "Right, was." He drained his beer abruptly, threw bills on the table and stood up.

"What's your hurry?" The poet was just getting a nice glow on and didn't feel like going back out into the cold just yet. "It's warm in here."

"We've *invited* people," Fussfaster said. Standing, he seemed to the poet to be squirming.

"Well, if you insist." The poet finished his drink and stood reluctantly. Fussfaster was already heading out to the car. The poet obediently fell in behind him, humming quietly to himself as he walked across the dark bar room. At the door an impulse seized him and he reached out to a potted plant, a large spidery fern, and pulled off some trailing leaves. Unnoticed, he rolled them up into a ball, put them in his mouth, chewed them briefly and swallowed them. The poet had no idea what kind of plant it was. The leaves tasted a little like mustard. He went out to the car and got in next to Fussfaster, who was already racing his motor. The bearded academic burned rubber, and they shot down a broad avenue toward the campus and residential part of town.

"Nice place," the poet said pleasantly. "Plants taste good, too."

"What's that?" Fussfaster said, suddenly lost in his own thoughts, no doubt of his wife's anger.

"I said it was a nice place, that bar."

"Oh. Yeah, it is."

They turned into a quiet side street of two-storey frame houses. Fussfaster pulled up in front of one of them and they got out.

Clare was waiting at the door with a false smile that twisted her face into strange formations. Rage burned in her otherwise colorless eyes. The poet surmised that she was one of those women who look best when they are furious. In her anger, she was a not unattractive woman, for an academic's wife. She wore a blue dress. The poet said hello to her and Fussfaster kissed her and apologized. "Plane was late," he said.

"Oh," she said, glaring at her husband. "The airport said it came in right on time." She turned to the poet. "Come in, won't you. I've got dinner all cooked."

They went inside. Five or six people—local literary types, the poet immediately guessed—were arrayed around Fussfaster's modern cedar-paneled living room, chatting and sipping wine. Clare introduced the poet to everyone and poured him a glass of expensive claret. He too sipped, smiled, chatted, making sure to float a few feet above the conversation as he did so. Presently Clare called them in to dinner, and they came, sat, and ate. The conversation continued. The women at the table talked to the poet, the men talked to each other for the poet's benefit, the poet made occasional comments to everyone and remarked to himself that he had had more interesting conversations with elm trees. Now and then he exchanged glances with Fussfaster's wife, who'd stopped acting angry once her dinner was consumed—if hastily, then at least with praise—and was, the poet noticed, staring at him almost greedily.

When dinner was over it was time to go. Clare sat between Fussfaster and the poet on the way to the reading. Fussfaster drove faster now that he was drunk. He passed on curves, took every corner with reckless abandon. The poet felt Clare's knee pressing against his. He pressed back, staring straight ahead. They ran a red light, shot up a one-way drive the wrong way, and screeched to a halt in the faculty lot behind the college's main auditorium and lecture hall. The poet felt Fussfaster's wife brush against him once again as they entered the building. Perhaps it was accidental. The poet looked up. Clare looked coolly into his eyes.

The reading went off like clockwork. Fussfaster performed the introduction, lauding the poet's works in eloquent English. Then the poet took the podium before a hushed audience of nearly four hundred people. The poet hated staid audiences, and so he now selected on the spur of the moment the most flagrant and obscene poem in his repertoire and launched into it in a loud and angry voice.

One by one, the more conservative members of the audience began leaving. Halfway into his poem, the poet noticed several dozen empty seats. This relaxed him. He paused, shrugged to show his disinterest, then smiled winningly and made a few amused comments before returning to his poem, which he now interpreted in a humorous, self-deprecating tone that drew scattered laughs all over the hall. By the end of it, the laughs had swelled into waves. Deftly seizing the moment, the poet then cracked an invisible whip with two short, tough lyrics that left the laughers stunned.

As always, he had things right on track. His hour-long reading grew and built in breadth and power. When it was done, there was an ovation that lasted a minute and a half.

After the reading a knot of cognoscenti formed at the foot of the stage. The less shy of his admirers came forth to shake the poet's hand. He exchanged a few meaningless words with everybody who wanted to talk, then began looking around for the Fussfasters, who were nowhere to be seen. He interrogated the hangers-on.

"They left for the party at Gordon White's house," a frizzy-haired student in rimless glasses announced. "David asked me to drive you over there."

"Who's Gordon White?" the poet asked.

"A rich guy who owns a lot of art and writes terrible poetry," the student said with a grin. A girl next to him giggled.

"Does he give good parties?" the poet asked.

"Oh, I guess so," the student said. "But we thought you might like to stop first at this *other* party. At this friend of ours' place."

"But what about Fussfaster and his wife, what's her name?"

"Clare. Don't worry. They won't miss us. We'll just stop off and get high and then go over to White's place."

"*If* you like to get high," the giggling girl put in.

"Don't know what you're talking about," the poet said, eyeing them severely. Then his face broke apart and he smiled broadly at the girl. "What the hell are we waiting for? Where's your goddam car?"

In the car to the first party someone handed the poet a joint.

"Thank you," he said, toking deeply.

At the party there were several women who struck the poet's fancy at once. There was also a man who kept laughing. Every time the poet said something, the man laughed.

When the host ran out of rolling papers, the poet suggested that

someone run down to the college library and pick up the Magna
Carta, since no one would be using it this late at night.

The laughing man laughed harder than ever.

The poet held up his hand, made a fist, then extended his index
finger to point at the laughing man, like the barrel of a pistol. The
poet sighted over it with his eye. "Bang," he said.

The laughing man went into hysterics.

The poet looked around the room. Six different women were
smiling at him at once, and he didn't know any of their names.

Some hours later, the poet was escorted to the home of Gordon
White, the wealthy dilettante who was throwing the principal party
of the evening.

White's colossal annual income from family businesses allowed
him to indulge freely his love of poetry. He hunted down precious
first editions, traveled hundreds of miles to attend readings by poets
whose work he liked, and had his own bad verses made into books.
After poetry, art was his second love, and he was a collector of
some stature. On the occasion of every large scale purchase, he
threw a party as a kind of private *vernissage*. Having recently ac-
quired a number of expensive works, he had chosen to share them
with friends on the evening of the poet's reading, thus combining
two celebrations. He had invited over a hundred people to join him
and his wife first at the reading, then afterwards at his home.

White's wife, Jane, was a pretty redhead young enough to be the
wealthy man's daughter. The poet felt her eyes on his as soon as he
entered the White's living room. Fussfaster, very drunk, rushed up
and with great fanfare introduced them; then Gordon White himself came up and took the poet's hand in a grasp no firmer than a
baby's. "Where have you been all evening?" White said. "Fine,
thanks," the poet said. Out of the corner of his eye he saw Clare
Fussfaster sitting on the lap of a tall white-haired man who looked
like Uncle Sam. While the poet watched, Clare bent down and
kissed the tip of the man's whiskers. The man grinned and deliberately spilled some of his drink down the back of her dress. She
squealed, jumped up and ran out of the room.

White had hired a pianist for the evening. A group of his guests

94

were now gathering around the piano to sing old songs. The poet moved out of earshot, relieved that he wouldn't be expected to make conversation during the musical offering. Looking back over his shoulder across the big living room, he saw his host leading the songfest, arms waving.

The poet wandered outside to the patio, where suddenly the lady of the house was standing in her evening gown in the snow, smoking and looking at the moon.

"Nice place you've got here," the poet said sociably.

"I suppose." Jane White's tone was tentative. "The snow is nice tonight."

"What's that building over there?" The poet nodded toward an imitation-adobe bungalow across the patio.

"Our guest house. And bath house, in the summer. The pool's on the other side of it, under those trees."

The poet could see a tall stand of cottonwoods beyond the guest house, their bare icy branches tracing a spidery outline in the moonlight.

"Bet it's nice over there in the summer."

"It is." She looked into the poet's eyes.

"Care to show me?"

She continued to look at him, her glance showing her uncertainty.

"I don't know."

"Oh, come on."

She smiled. "Well, all right." She threw her cigarette into the snow.

The poet took her arm and they walked toward the dark guest house in the moonlight.

From the big house behind them, the muffled vocalism of a dozen untalented throats assaulted the snowy silence of the night.

When the singing ended, the host noticed his wife's absence, and went around the room asking everyone if they'd seen her. Embarrassed negatives and blank stares were the only answer he got. It didn't take a detective to figure out that the poet had also vanished.

Fingering the spines of some of his rare books, White stood for a moment by his bookshelves, his back to his guests, thinking. Then abruptly he turned, lurched across the room and out the front door into the snow, carrying in his hand a slim book of poetry. He left the door wide open behind him, so that his guests could watch his diminutive swaying progress across the patio until his image disappeared into the snow. People exchanged sympathetic glances and went on drinking.

Jane drove. She and the poet were headed deep into the heart of the American night, out of town, up through the snow into the mountains. She had a cabin up there. They would spend the night: that was her plan. She talked and smoked while she drove.

As they climbed the hills above the town, they noticed headlights behind them. She slowed down to let the other car pass, but it slowed down too.

"We're being followed," she said.

"By who?" the poet asked.

"It's Gordon. I'm sure of it."

"He read your mind?"

"I'm afraid so."

"What do we do?"

She stepped on the gas, the rear of the car swaying as the wheels worked to get traction on the slick road.

The poet could no longer see the moon. They were passing through dense pine forest, tall dark trees rising on both sides of the road as they climbed. The headlights of the dillettante's car stayed close behind them.

"Is he alone?" the poet asked.

"I don't know. Probably. Nobody would come with him."

They kept climbing. It was hard to see the road. Light snow was beginning to fall. Jane had to slow down. Her husband followed doggedly.

They came to the top of a pass, and Jane turned off onto a side road that led into dark trees. She followed this for a few minutes, then turned again. At last the headlights bounced off something bright: twin reflectors. A driveway. She pulled in. Her husband pulled in behind them.

Jane and the poet sat in her car with the lights on. Behind them in the driveway, White did the same.

"Now what?" the poet asked.

Jane sighed. "He's watching us. No, now he's getting out."

The poet heard crunching footsteps in the snow. The footsteps came up closer, on his side of the car. He looked out. Gordon White was there, holding something out. The object in the dilettante's hand flashed bright in the car lights. The poet flinched, figuring he was about to be shot in the head.

There was no explosion, no flash.

The poet looked again.

White was waving a book at him. A thin book with a white cover.

It was the poet's latest volume of poems.

He rolled down his window.

White thrust the book through the window, into the poet's hands.

"Please," White said. "Sign this, won't you?"

The poet shook his head, truly confused.

"You don't have a pen? Here." White fished in his pockets, brought out a pen and handed it to the poet, who held it delicately as if it might ignite spontaneously.

"You want me to sign this book?" he said, awed.

White nodded excitedly. His eyes were wide, avid. He did not even glance across the front seat at his wife on the driver's side, but kept on gazing at the poet.

The poet opened the book and began to write on the title page.

"Make it 'To Gordon,' would you?" White said softly.

The poet obligingly scribbled a few lines and handed the book back.

White took it and grinned apologetically into the car. "I'm sorry if my following you upset you," he said. "I didn't want you to get away without signing this for me. I know you've got an early plane and all."

The poet nodded, still stunned.

"Well, have a nice evening," White said, glancing toward the cabin whose outlines the poet could barely make out at the top of the driveway. "I put a new stove in last winter, and there's wood stacked by the kitchen door." Standing in the swirling snow, holding the poetry book, he continued to smile into his wife's car idiotically.

"Thanks a lot," the poet said.

White murmured something inaudible, turned, and staggered back to his car. The motor was still running. He got in, backed down the driveway, and a moment later had disappeared into the mountain night.

"He really likes your poems," Jane said in a tone of simple explanation. "Tonight will mean a lot to him."

"It will?"

"Sure. He'll be proud to show his friends that dedication. They were all very impressed with your reading, you know."

"Ah," the poet said, trying to take in this information. It had been a long evening.

"Well, let's not just sit here all night," Jane said, switching off the lights. "I'm getting cold. What say we go inside and get a fire going?"

The poet followed her inside, his shoes making noises like popcorn in the snow.

In the morning he was on a plane to San Francisco.

Incident at Basecamp

The wind blew harder and harder. It came from the west, from vacant expanses of the Great Basin. It rose swiftly to vault the mountains, and then swooped down the other side, often with hurricane force, rolling along the Rockies' eastern slope in great waves whose strength and behavior resembled the huge breakers generated by a Pacific squall.

In the six months the Stanleys had been living in the mountains, they had heard many stories about Basecamp's famed winter wind, which according to local legend blew down out of the Divide with enough force to lift the roof off any house in town that wasn't built like a fortress.

The Stanleys' ranch house had once been a miner's cabin. The ancient timbers and masonry were still visible at two or three points in the kitchen wall, which had been painstakingly reconstructed to resemble the original. The house was much bigger and solider now, with electricity and piped water and gas, but there was a feel of primitive design about the place that connected it more convincingly with gold rush days than with the mundane present. It was a feeling none of the amenities of the place could dispel, and it was stronger at night when you couldn't look out the window and see a pickup truck and a red Volkswagen parked in the driveway. At night, the place returned to the past where it had come from. This return was most dramatic and distracting on nights when the wind blew.

The whole place hummed and banged and buzzed then, and the more it happened the more certain Mike Stanley became that there were other than simple natural forces behind all the racket. It seemed like some second power was accelerating the wind in just this one spot, the small canyon where their house was. Mike had never experienced wind like this before; neither had his wife. There was so much electricity in the air—everyone who came into the house during one of the windstorms immediately commented on it. The whole house seemed to be humming, as though an extraordinary current were passing through it. Mike checked all the wiring, re-checked it, then went over it one more time just to make sure he wasn't missing anything. He tried every circuit in the house three times. It all checked out perfectly, only the humming continued—every time the wind blew. And the harder the wind blew, the louder the house hummed.

There was a windstorm in August, none in September, one in October, several in late November. In early December it began to blow in earnest. The Stanleys could tell winter was coming on for real, then, because the inhabitants of Basecamp began to stay at home. You saw few people in the streets, only an occasional car, no one on foot. It snowed heavily, then snowed again, and the wind picked up the dry snow and swirled it in eddies of icy particles that stung the face if one ventured out into it. As the temperature dipped below zero and the snow and wind increased, the Stanleys emulated their neighbors and stopped going outside at all, except for the few steps it required to get to the car from the house and vice versa.

*

Mike's company had transferred him from New York to its Denver office in May. He had come west ahead of time to find a place. The air in Denver was too bad for him to consider moving his family there, he quickly decided. Since he would be doing much of his work at home and would be required to spend only a few days a week in the office, he felt it would be best to find a place out of the city. Helen and the boys shared his love of the outdoors and nature. Here was an opportunity for them all to enjoy a beautiful part of the country. Mike's company referred him to a realtor who gave him a line on available mountain properties up and down the Front Range. Mike and the realtor made several visits to each of the small mountain communities he had in mind. On one such trip, to the Basecamp area, the realtor told him about a place that had just gone on the market, an enlarged and remodeled miner's cabin. It had been vacant for two years, the realtor said, and now the owner had died and his heirs were interested in making a quick sale. Their asking price and terms were well within Mike's range, so he agreed to take a look. The realtor drove him up to the place one sparkling day in early May.

100

There were still piles of old snow lying among the abundant wild flowers in the corral along the entry road, which was lined with aspens on both sides. A stream ran alongside the road. On either side, red rock canyon walls rose steeply to stands of tall pine whose green-black tops punctuated a lucid cobalt sky. Jays and squirrels chattered. Mike and the realtor walked up the flagstone driveway to the house. Mike had made up his mind to take the place before they reached the front door.

*

Helen Stanley put the boys to bed, washed her hair, and sat down on a sofa by the fire with a cup of coffee and a book. It was the middle of December. Mike was away for a few days on a business trip to the West Coast. Earlier in the evening he had called from San Francisco and promised the boys that he would take them out into the woods to cut a Christmas tree as soon as he got back. It was a Thursday night, and he would be flying home the next afternoon.

"We'll go out with the ax first thing Sunday morning," he told them. "We'll find the best tree in the canyon."

"Yippee!" said the boys.

Helen got on the line next, and assured her husband that she was fine, that all was well at home, and that she would have dinner ready for him if he thought he'd be back in time.

"Don't expect me before eight," Mike said. "I've got a five-thirty plane, but you never know about the weather this time of year. How's it been back there?"

"Windy, a little," Helen said. "It could be a storm coming." She listened with one ear to the humming that was already beginning to fill the house. A major blow was getting underway.

"Well, batten down the hatches, and I'll be home ahead of it if we're lucky."

After she talked to Mike, the wind picked up, and drafts were whistling around in the roof beams. Helen shivered and huddled closer to the fire. Mike had cut half a cord of wood before leaving, and there were three large logs blazing in the grate now. Even so, Helen

101

felt chilled. Perhaps it was her wet hair. She tried to concentrate on her book, but kept feeling an odd sensation on the back of her neck. She reached to touch her neck, and was surprised to find that her hair was not only completely dry, but standing on end. "Electrostatic effects," she told herself. "It's that damn wind." She shook her hair out, long blonde tresses that were her pride and joy. As she did so, she heard—or rather, felt—a strange buzzing in the air around her. At that moment the lights in the house went out. The chills sprang down her neck and gripped her spine.

By the firelight Helen could see clearly enough. Her first thought was to go and get candles. But a funny malaise held her. Why get more light? It was bright enough to see, wasn't it? She didn't feel like moving—something told her not to. She knew she should be checking the fuses to find the source of the power failure. *But she couldn't get up.* The house groaned and creaked, its wooden frame yielding minutely to the terrific gusts. There was that buzzing again—Helen glanced quickly at the fire, which was burning normally. The crackling continued, and there was the loudest humming Helen had ever heard. She clutched her ears. The humming noise followed her inside her head and increased till she grew nauseous, dizzy, feared she would pass out. Then it stopped completely. So did the wind and the buzzing. The room was silent except for the light crackling sounds of the fire. Helen's eyes moved slowly around the room. She felt paralyzed, frozen stiff with apprehension—and something more. Someone or something was watching her, she was certain.

Then the lights went back on.

*

Helen told Mike about what had happened as soon as he got back. Mike listened intently but said only "I'm glad to be home." They ate dinner and discussed his trip.

In the morning, when Mike took the boys out to chop down a Christmas tree, he brought along his rifle. It was a cold, still, grey morning; there were several inches of new snow that packed down and squeaked under their boots as they walked through the woods at the foot of the steep canyon wall. There were some small firs growing

102

in among the aspens. Mike let the boys pick one out, and he chopped it down. They started back.

The boys took the lead on the way home. Mike fell in step behind them, keeping his eyes and ears open. His perceptive powers felt enhanced, sensitized—he heard every twig break, saw every movement of snow dropping from a branch. Ten yards ahead of him the boys walked, chatting, their breath making pale balloons in the steely air. The boys weren't going fast, but for some reason Mike felt himself slipping behind. He felt winded, suddenly tired. He was going to call out to the boys to hold up and wait for him, but a sound behind him made him turn instead. The sound was high pitched and mechanical. What he saw when he turned around stopped him dead in his tracks.

A creature was standing in a small clearing five yards away from him, watching him. The creature was about five-and-a-half feet tall, human in appearance, but with extraordinarily large eyes, and was wearing a skin-tight suit and hood of some luminous, liquid-like material. The creature held up one hand and beckoned for Mike to approach. Forgetting the boys, Mike walked toward the creature, compelled not only by a power he didn't understand, but also by his own very strong curiosity. He felt no fear at all.

Suddenly a voice like a loudspeaker went on in Mike's head.

"Come this way," the voice said.

"All right," Mike heard himself saying. He could hardly believe he was saying this.

"There is no danger," said the voice. "We mean you no harm."

"I know," Mike said. "I feel that."

The creature turned and walked briskly into the woods. Mike dropped his ax and rifle and followed, hurrying to keep up. In less than a hundred yards they had reached the canyon wall. The creature turned toward the north and slowed down, picking his way through the trees, motioning for Mike to stay behind him. They came to a spot Mike had passed two or three times when he was out walking. The canyon wall was heavily overgrown with underbrush. Through the tangled branches a mine shaft opening could be seen. Mike had been tempted to enter, when he'd come here before, but something—fear of the dark, claustrophobia, all those things that

make mine shafts frightening—had prevented him. Now the creature walked through the undergrowth as if it didn't exist and passed
into the dark shaft. Mike, a few steps behind, had to struggle to get
through the undergrowth; as he did so, he saw the branches tearing
his clothing and cutting into his skin, but he felt nothing.

Inside the dark tunnel, the going was slow. There was ice under-
foot, and the narrow-gauge rails were in bad disrepair. Beams jutted
down into the tunnel, and several times Mike bumped into them. At
one point he tripped over a pile of fallen rock. After the first turn,
there was no light at all. Mike was able to proceed only by the
reflected light of the creature's suit, moving ahead of him like a torch.

Suddenly the footing became solid, the ground flat and hard; Mike
heard his steps echoing in what must have been a fairly large subterranean chamber. There was another turn, and the darkness fell away
abruptly. Ahead of them there was a bright greenish light. The
creature was leading Mike down a broad corridor with a ceiling a few
feet above Mike's head and walls about ten feet apart. The walls,
floor and ceiling seemed to be made of some very hard metal; Mike
could hear his own footsteps ring out like small caliber gunshots. The
creature's tread was much lighter, softer, by comparison; its feet
seemed to be encased in soft pads instead of shoes.

The greenish light grew in brilliance and intensity until they appeared to be only a few yards away from its source. Mike felt his face
bathed in a pleasant warmth, first; then as they came closer, the heat
became quite strong, and he felt it searing his skin. The feeling was
not painful—more like an objective perception that someone else's
face was being burned. The creature stopped, and motioned for
Mike to do the same.

The field of greenish light before them suddenly turned bright
white. Mike shielded his eyes, but not in time to prevent himself
from being temporarily blinded. He fell to his knees, and lost consciousness.

The next thing he knew he was on his feet again, naked, inside
some kind of glass chamber. He could not move. The air around him
was not air at all, but some kind of viscous gel of high density—a kind
of aerated plastic, Mike guessed. It held him, encased, as a block of
ice would have. Yet he could breathe, and see quite clearly. Through

104

the transparent gel he could see other glass boxes, with people and large animals in them, arranged in rows in the large cargo hold of what appeared to be some kind of ship. The people and animals in the other boxes were all "frozen" solid in the clear plastic gel, held as Mike was in a state of suspended animation. All of them, several elk and deer, two cows, a mountain lion, and three young humans (two girls in their twenties, one Eurasian, one Caucasian, and a teenage boy with Hispanic features) had their eyes wide open and were looking anxiously at one another as Mike was at them. There was eye movement; it was clear all of the captives were conscious.

Captives. Mike's brain began to clear. His memory pushed a wild series of images to the forefront of his mind—pictures of himself on a table that moved, being probed and touched by instruments in the hands of . . . he dismissed the images and tried to grasp the present situation. He was a captive. He had dropped his rifle and ax and followed the creature—why? How in his right mind, could he have abandoned the boys like that? Something had come over him—the voice in his head. So pleasant and intelligent, he hadn't been able to resist. Here he was in a glass box on the inside of some kind of a ship. Frozen solid in clear gelatin. How was he going to get back?

Between the rows of boxes there ran narrow aisles. Down one of these Mike saw two creatures approaching on foot. One was the human-looking creature with the pleasant voice who'd invited him to follow, back in the forest. The other was taller, thinner, pale, with a huge helmeted head and shiny appliances on his chest. They stopped at each box and examined the contents. When they got to Mike's box, a voice went on in Mike's head. The tall spindly creature was peering at him intently. The human-looking creature studied him also, with a look that Mike couldn't help thinking was apologetic.

"Welcome," said the voice in Mike's head. It was the same voice he had heard in the forest.

"Welcome to *what?*" Mike said to himself.

The voice seemed to have heard his thought. "To our ship," it said.

Mike formed another question in his mind, this time more deliberately. "Am I a prisoner?"

"Correct." This voice was a new one. High-pitched, metallic.

Evidently it came from the tall spindly creature, who was still peering at him with total concentration, its large eyes moving slowly from feature to feature.

Mike's mind felt cloudy. He tried to think about the boys. Were they—

"They are safe," the pleasant voice said.

Mike began to relax. He felt himself being lulled. There were so many things he wanted to ask—but he couldn't make the thoughts clear. His mind kept drifting. He wanted to ask whether the ship was moving, where they were going. . . .

"You will sleep now," said the high metallic voice. A membrane flickered over each of the spindly creature's large eyes, which were aimed directly into Mike's. It was a stare like none other Mike had ever felt—it seemed to engulf him, to pull his mind out through his eyes. His head felt drained. He could barely remember what his sons looked like. . . .

"They are safe," the pleasant voice repeated.

Mike fell asleep.

The two creatures passed on to the next glass box.

*

When the boys came back without their father, Helen phoned the sheriff, who told her not to worry. Disappearances were "routine" in this part of the country, the lawman said. Most of them were merely temporary. "If your husband isn't back by morning, Mrs. Stanley, call me again and I'll see what I can do about finding him."

Helen couldn't believe her ears. "What do you mean, disappearances are routine?"

There was a brief silence, then the sheriff cleared his throat. "A lot of people, er, turn up missing."

"But *why?*"

"Nobody knows, ma'am. They just step out of the picture for an hour or two, then they show up again—usually with no idea where they've been. Total amnesia."

"You're joking."

"No, ma'am."

106

"Well, I hope you're not suggesting my husband—"

"Some of 'em come back with marks on 'em."

"Marks?"

"On their foreheads, backs, arms. You know—rashes, ma'am. Small bruises. Nothing serious."

"Officer, what are you trying to suggest?"

"I ain't suggesting *nothin'*, ma'am. Just telling you about these disappearances we've been getting. Now if you figure your husband just run out on you—"

"That's ridiculous." Helen's voice rose in anger.

"Well, then, what you're saying is your husband just *vanished*, ma'am. And *I'm* just saying it's been happening to a lot of people hereabouts. But it's no cause for worry, because like I say most of 'em are back in an hour or two."

"*Most?* What happens to the others?"

"Well, ma'am, one or two of these disappearance people have been able to remember a *few* things about what happened to 'em. They say they were picked up by some kind of funny characters and put through a lot of tests. 'They didn't want us,' they say. 'We were rejected.'"

"Officer, if this is a joke you're going too far. I want you to help me find my husband."

"Call me in the morning, ma'am." The phone went dead.

"Damn!" Helen jammed the receiver down angrily, then saw that her two boys were watching her with anxious looks. "You guys go and let me use the phone, will you?" She tried to smile. The boys exchanged concerned glances and wandered off toward their room.

She picked up the phone again and called Buck Warburton, Mike's business partner and their old friend. They'd told Buck all about the queer goings-on at the ranch. Now, when Helen told him what had happened—that Mike was missing—Buck agreed to drive up immediately, despite the snow.

*

As Buck drove he played with his CB radio, trying to pick up first hand weather reports on the road ahead. He tuned in a stay-at-home in Eagle, where it was snowing heavily, then a guy on the road near Wolf Lake, who'd just come down from Basecamp and told Buck there was a lot of wind up that way, and "enough ice on the road to keep all the beer in Colorado cold."

At the Echo Creek turnoff a state police officer was standing at the mouth of Echo Pass Road, warning cars off. Buck took the country road instead, negotiating slick curves all the way to Roberts, then made the steep uphill turn toward Basecamp. By the time he reached the east end of the valley he could see the town lights glimmering ahead of him; it was getting dark. The thick snowflakes looked blue in his headlights. The sky turned from menacing grey to black, and Buck and his headlights were alone in the gloom of a high altitude snowstorm. Fearful of the ice that he could feel through his tires under the new-fallen powder snow, he kept to a stolid twenty-or-so miles per hour. Despite his excitement—Helen had sounded half-hysterical—he wanted to make sure to reach the ranch in one piece.

Headlights appeared in the opposite lane, approaching from the west end of the valley (which led straight up to the Divide). They were very bright. Buck flashed his own brights, twice, but the oncoming lights just got brighter and brighter. Much too fast, Buck thought.

Then suddenly the lights were one light, and it was orange, with a bluish-green trail, and it was not on the road at all. It was in the sky, traveling very swiftly over the valley from west to east. As it went over Buck's car he heard a dull *whooshing* sound, and sensed in the dark a great black volume enclosed by the bright field of light. He hit the brakes, unthinking. The car skidded in the ice, and swerved out of its lane onto the opposite shoulder and into a ditch. Buck sprang out, unhurt, and looked up into the sky. The lights had turned and were moving off toward the south at unbelievable speed. In a moment they had left the valley.

It took Buck forty minutes to reach Basecamp on foot, and another hour to hike through the snowstorm up to the ranch. Not a single car passed him; it was no night to be out.

Helen opened the door warily, then burst into tears when she saw Buck. He hugged her and shut the door on the storm.

"Mike still isn't back," she said. She sounded and looked very shaky.

"What about the boys?"

"I finally convinced them to go to bed."

"Good. Got any coffee?"

"Of course—I'm sorry. You look like you could use it." Buck's eyebrows and mustache were coated with ice.

"Make it black."

They went into the kitchen. Over coffee, Helen told Buck where Mike had last been seen—near the canyon wall, "around those old mine shafts."

"What'd the boys say, again?"

"They said they got a little ahead and looked back and he was just gone. They carried the Christmas tree back by themselves." Helen nodded toward a corner of the kitchen, where the slender young fir was propped.

"So what do *you* think happened?" Buck asked.

Helen told him what the sheriff had said.

Buck thought for a minute and then asked for the largest flashlight the Stanleys owned.

"Oh, and does Mike keep a hand gun by any chance?"

Helen nodded. "It's in the top drawer of our dresser, in the bedroom."

"Why don't you go and get it."

While Helen went to get the flashlight and gun, Buck finished his coffee and buttoned up his coat, which he hadn't taken off. Helen came back and handed him the long-handled flash and a small snubnosed .32 pistol. Buck slipped the gun into his pocket, took the flash and got ready to step back out into the storm.

"I'd like to come with you," Helen said as hopefully as she could.

"Better if you stay here with the boys." Buck's tone was final.

He pulled the door open and went out, pushing it shut behind him with effort. The wind was coming up.

After Buck left, the gusts increased. Helen felt the house begin to hum and buzz, groan and shudder. She poured herself another cup of coffee, went into the living room and sat down in front of the fire to wait. Her heart was pounding so loud it almost kept her from hearing the wind.

*

The town of Basecamp in December resembled a country village in Russia, most of its windows boarded over for the season, only a few sparse spires of smoke rising from its chimneys. A normal Basecamp winter was only slightly more eventful than a winter spent on the moon.

What night life there was centered around the Frontier Bar, a primitive establishment on Main Street which supported two country and western bands nightly, during the summer tourist season, and stayed open all winter not because it was profitable but because its owner, Joe Beauregard, enjoyed the company the place provided him. Some years ago Joe had gone south for a winter, and upon his return swore he would never allow the word "Florida" to be uttered in his presence again. "Nothin' but goddam clip joints and fairies," he said. "It's good to be home where a man's a man."

On this particular evening in December seven residents of Basecamp were weathering the storm at the bar of the Frontier. Joe, on the serving side, chatted across the polished hardwood with two of his best customers and buddies, Spencer Workman and Darrell Driver. Spencer and Darrell were employed at a local lumber mill in the summer and fall, and by the Basecamp Municipal Water Company the rest of the year. It was they who dug up frozen water pipes during blizzards in January. They did so with great quantities of whiskey and delight. Both had been born and raised in the region, had attended Basecamp School together and had even managed to wind up in the same unit in Vietnam—and to survive. The latter development had convinced them that their friendship was preordained by destiny.

Next to Spencer and Darrell, drinking alone, was old Hiram

Rowder, a hoary former miner who still lived in the cabin he'd been born and married in—hard by the mouth of the Happy Valley Mine, to which his pappy had come from West Virginia to work as a hard rock miner in 1888. Hiram muttered and snorted into his shot of rye, re-telling to himself the dirty stories of a lifetime. Every now and then he laughed quietly, a faraway look passed over his eyes and he vanished into the past, leaving only his crooked old body behind him.

At Hiram's side, the sheriff, George De Silva, sipped a beer in silence, a thoughtful look crinkling his thick brows.

Beyond the sheriff, on isolated stools down near the end of the bar, two young people talked together seriously as they drank. Tommy Berglund, who wore his hair in a pony tail and lived a shoestring solitary existence in one of the oldest, most dilapidated cabins in town, had a lady friend everybody in town liked. Eileen Watts was her name, and he sat talking with her now. Eileen worked in a bank in Denver and came out to visit Tommy and stay at the cabin whenever she had a few days off. Her Christmas vacation had begun, and she was staying at Tommy's for the holidays. Eileen was cheerful, friendly, and pretty in the bony kind of way the mountain boys liked. In the summer Tommy always had a hard time keeping drunks away from her. In the winter, Basecamp believed in live and let live. The elements were too extreme to allow for much rowdiness; men who got drunk and fought brawls in the snow often wound up falling in deep drifts unnoticed, passing out and freezing to death. Basecamp was not an easy place in winter. Folks generally behaved themselves and concentrated on surviving.

Hiram was cackling about something. George De Silva got the feeling Hiram was trying to tell him something. George looked up slowly from his drink.

"What's that, Hiram?"

"I said I saw one of them goddam things again. Tonight, just now."

"What things?"

"You know damn well what things."

"Ah."

Hiram leered, then scowled, coughed, and spat a dark wad onto

111

the sawdust floor.

"Some law officer you are."

"I just do my job, Hiram."

"'N I suppose them damn space ships ain't part of your job?"

"Hiram, I don't know what you're talking about." The sheriff spoke deliberately, looking straight ahead and sipping his beer with great delicacy.

"Ha!" Hiram croaked in triumph, and swallowed his shot.

Joe Beauregard had been listening. He took two steps down the bar and smiled patronizingly at Hiram, half-humoring the old man. Joe knew all about Hiram's space ship stories—and everybody else's. He hadn't "seen one" himself but he supposed them to be real. Why would his customers lie to him?

"What do you think they're after, Hiram?"

"Ha. I *know* what they're after." Hiram was playing coy.

Joe got out a bottle from under the bar and tipped it over Hiram's glass. By now Spencer and Darrell were listening and interested.

"That's it, Joe, oil the old boy up," Darrell said.

"Come on, Hiram," Darrell coaxed. "We're your pals, ain't we? Tell us what them dang spacemen are up to!" He slapped Hiram on the back.

The old man coughed and exhaled half his drink in a spray across the bar. Joe had to get out a towel to wipe it up. Down the bar, Tommy and Eileen looked up at the commotion.

Hiram was sputtering. Joe refilled his glass. Then Hiram began to talk, as everyone at the bar hoped he would.

"It's the mines," he said.

"The mines, Hiram?" Joe leaned forward on the bar, chin on palm, eyes sparkling.

"You're goddam right, the mines. That's what they want. I've seen 'em. They go down in there. All the old tunnels—they're working those old mines."

Joe's face dropped. "Working 'em?"

"You heard me." Hiram threw back another shot as soon as Joe poured it. "Excuse me, boys." He got up, wobbly.

"Aw, c'mon, Hiram," Spencer said, grabbing the old man's arm and pulling him back down on the stool. "You don't mean to tell us those space folks are really *mining* them old holes?"

Hiram shook his head; he'd say no more. He struggled out of Spencer's grasp and staggered toward the door. Just before going out into the storm he stopped and looked back significantly.

"I been down in them holes myself," Hiram said. He tapped the side of his head with one finger. "I been down there with a *geiger counter.*" Then he pulled his ragged coat tight around his frail chest and lurched outside.

*

Tommy and Eileen were walking home. Tommy's cabin was just off Main Street, so they didn't have far to go. It was snowing hard, in thick, dense flakes. The wind was starting to blow, and the chill flakes drove into their faces. Tommy pulled his scarf up over his face and tucked Eileen's shoulder under his arm to shield her from the wind. Thus united, they stumbled along happily. They'd had four glasses of beer apiece and were feeling a rosy glow that kept out the cold.

"What a character, that old Hiram," Tommy chuckled as they walked.

"Yeah, I love him," Eileen said.

"He's sure got a thing going about the space people, hasn't he?"

Eileen laughed. Then her voice turned serious. "What do you think he meant about the geiger counter?"

"Oh, he's always saying there's uranium down in the old Happy Valley and the other mines around here. A big vein of it."

"*Is* there?" Eileen wasn't laughing now.

"Well, if there is, I guess Hiram ought to know. He spent his whole life around here—worked down in 'em and everything."

"And if there *is* uranium—" Eileen stopped short.

Tommy's voice rose as he injected it with mock dramatics. "And if the *spacemen* are after it—"

Eileen wrenched out of Tommy's grasp and plowed on ahead through the snow, alone for a moment.

"Hey, what'd I do?" Tommy took two long strides and caught up.

113

"I don't see why you make such a joke out of everything," Eileen said.

"Hey, I take Hiram seriously. You know that."

Eileen looked up at Tommy, smiled through the storm. Her breath blossomed in a small steam cloud. She went to speak, then stopped and pressed up against her friend again. They walked home through the snow, huddled together closely, their steps making a crackling, crunching music on the foot of hard-pack that always covered Basecamp's side streets this time of year.

Back at Tommy's cabin, Eileen made hot cocoa and toast. They sat in the humble kitchen at a pine table Tommy had made himself, out of beetle kill from behind the cabin. It was the first piece of furniture he'd ever built and he was proud of it.

When the cocoa was finished, Tommy lit up a joint, and they had just begun smoking it when there was a loud banging noise, like someone pounding on the outside wall of the cabin. Tommy dropped the joint and jumped to his feet, knocking his tin cup off the table. The cup clattered to the floor. Then there was silence.

"What was *that?*" Eileen said softly, her eyes wide.

"You got me," said Tommy, crossing the kitchen on cat's feet. He could feel himself trembling. As he neared the wall, the banging happened again. Tommy stopped dead in his tracks. Silence again.

"Tommy," Eileen said.

He went back to the table and sat down beside her and put his arm around her. Together they waited—a few seconds, a few more, and then there was more banging, and a high-pitched noise that sounded like a laugh.

"Damn!" Eileen hissed. "I bet it's that Spencer and Darrell."

Tommy's mind raced. The thought of harassment by the two town rowdies frightened him even more than his first thought, which was to suspect the spacemen.

They waited again, frozen. Something moved in front of them. They looked up. The kitchen door, which was four inches thick and made of solid wood, was coalescing. It liquefied, fluttered like cellophane, shimmered like some translucent membrane. Tommy wondered if he was going out of his mind. He looked at Eileen. Her

114

face was white, her eyes enormous. Her fingernails were digging into Tommy's arm. She saw it too.

The door fluttered for what must have been three or four minutes. Then it turned back into a door. Eileen's grip on Tommy's arm relaxed. Tommy began to weep. He couldn't help himself.

They went to bed and held each other in the dark, awake all night, talking and talking. Whatever had come to visit them did not come back.

*

The snow piled up, higher and higher under Buck Warburton's boots as he slogged across the canyon floor toward the old mine shaft. He knew that spot well; he'd hiked there with Mike many times. But he'd never walked this way at night, or in deep snow. So he went slowly, probing the trees with his light, one gloved hand in his pocket clutching the butt of Mike's .32. There were sometimes bears in these woods in winter, Buck knew. He sensed that on this night there also might be something else.

The furry thing peered out from behind a tree. It saw in infra-red. It "saw" Buck coming by sensing him as an approaching heat-field. To divert itself it mimed his cautious stride, lifting its nether paws daintily in and out of the deep snow, one dorsal paw thrust into the fur at its hip in imitation of Buck's gun hand, the other dorsal paw held out ahead as if holding a flashlight. It was a perfect imitation.

As Buck came closer, the furry thing lifted a black metal box which had been resting at its feet. The box emitted a beam of light and a faint hum. The hum increased in depth as Buck approached, growing to a heavy rumbling growl like that of some large piece of malfunctioning machinery.

Buck saw the light and heard the growl at just about the same time, and in the next moment he was on his belly in the snow, the .32 thrust out in front of him, aiming it through the darkness at the light and noise that were coming out of the trees ahead.

The noise stayed constant, a steady hum. The glowing box sent its beam into Buck's eyes. He felt himself growing drowsy. No.

Mustn't. . . . He struggled to his feet, dropping his flashlight into the snow, and staggered away from the growling, glowing light-box into the dark woods.

It took Buck two hours to find his way back to the ranch in the snow. All the way, the furry thing followed him, miming him, letting out an occasional high-pitched metallic laugh.

*

Inside his block of liquid plexiglass, or whatever it was that enclosed him, Mike slept and woke. The creature with the pleasant voice, the one he had first encountered in the woods, came around to see him again. This time the creature's voice inside his head was harder to pick up, because there was a heavy rumbling sound that interfered with it.

Mike wondered what the noise was.

"We are moving," said the voice inside his head.

A chill ran down Mike's spine. Would he ever see the earth again?

"We are not going far," the creature informed him. Mike thought the voice had a reassuring tone. Was the creature trying to be friendly?

"Our attitude toward all beings is benign," the voice said. On the creature's face there was no expression, except a movement of the eyes, possibly a kind of smile?

Mike formed a new question: where are we going?

"Our mission on your planet is scientific," the voice said. "We have received orders to proceed to another sector for sampling."

"Sampling?"

"You will see."

"And then what?"

"Then we have other orders."

"Such as?" There was that chill again.

"This craft has a finite fuel pack. After a specified period of time we must return to our base for refueling. This period, in your calendar, is only about six months. We will be returning to our base in a few days. First this sampling must be done; then we come back here; then we proceed to our base."

116

"Where is that?"

"In another part of your solar system."

"Do I go with you?" Mike's thought was frantic.

"Of course," the creature said. "Do you imagine we'd be telling you this if you were not returning with us?"

"If you're so benign toward all beings, what about asking me if I *want* to come?"

"*Do* you want to accompany us?"

"You're damn right I don't!"

"That is too bad." The creature's voice sounded disappointed inside Mike's head.

"I've got a family, and—"

"We understand. The decision about your fate is made by others."

"Which others?"

"We have chains of command. There are others who have observed you."

"That tall spindly thing?"

The creature nodded. "I must go now." He motioned toward a dark area at the far end of the cargo hold. Mike could see that end of the hold without moving.

"When we land again, you will be able to observe your planet through a viewing aperture there." The creature took three or four steps down the aisle toward the next box.

"Wait!" Mike cried out in his mind.

The creature stopped and looked back at him.

"What's this stuff you've got me frozen in?"

"Nothing," the creature said.

"Nothing?"

"You are being held in a vacuum. You are safe and protected from all entropic effects."

"You mean there's nothing in this tank at all?"

"Correct."

"Then why can't I move?"

The creature displayed the smile-like eye movement again, then turned and walked away.

*

In the morning, when Mike still hadn't returned, Helen called George De Silva again.

George drove out to the ranch and talked to Buck, who was in a state of high excitement about his experiences of the night before, and to Helen, who was terrified about what had become of her husband.

"Can't you at least go out to the old mines and *look?*" she begged.

"There's an awful lot of snow out there." The sheriff sounded hesitant.

"Look here, De Silva," Buck said, "you got to do *something.*"

"I don't know as how I ought to go out there alone." George De Silva sounded worried.

"We'll get up a goddamned *posse*, then," Buck exclaimed. "There's a man *lost* out there in this snow, sheriff!"

"Calm down, man," De Silva said. "Let me make a couple of phone calls."

Helen handed the sheriff a telephone. He dialed a local number.

"Spencer? This is George. You and Darrell busy this morning?"

There was a pause. George nodded. "Yes, well, old Bill Walters can wait a couple of hours to get his pipes unstuck. I need some help out here at the Stanley place. I know it's cold, but I'd sure appreciate it if you and Darrell could run out here for a couple of hours."

Apparently Spencer had agreed, because George was grinning when he hung up.

"We'll get to the bottom of this as soon as we can," he said, looking from Buck to Helen and trying to sound reassuring. "Meanwhile, is there any coffee going?"

Twenty minutes later the two strapping young men from the Basecamp Municipal Water Department arrived at the ranch in their yellow pickup truck.

"Best snow tires in town," Darrell boasted as he shook the snow off his coat.

"Damn right," Spencer echoed. "Ain't a road in this state can stop us."

"Well, boys, I hope you're ready for a little walking," George De Silva said.

118

"Yep," Darrell grinned. "We're set to go, sheriff. Who we lookin' for? Some real mean low-down criminals?"

"We brought weapons," Spencer chimed in. "Got our huntin' guns out in the truck."

"Take it easy, boys," George De Silva said. "We're looking for Mike Stanley, who got himself lost out there in the snow. If you bring them weapons along, I want you to make sure you don't use 'em until you get the word from me. That goes for you, too," he glanced at Buck. "That furry thing you saw, I've seem 'em too. They turn up on a lot of these disappearance cases. I've talked to the FBI about 'em, I've talked to the Air Force. They all tell me the same thing. 'Don't worry,' they tell me. 'We know what they are and what they're up to. Just don't shoot at 'em and you'll be all right.'"

"What the hell you talkin' about, George?" Spencer looked baffled. "What furry thing?"

"Don't worry, boys. Nothin' out of the ordinary." George sounded unconvincing.

"What kinda bizarre activities you got goin' on here, folks?" Darrell glanced questioningly from Buck to Helen and back.

Nobody said anything for a moment, until George made a movement for the door.

"Well, boys, either we got a search party here or we don't."

He went out, with Buck, Darrell and Spencer following.

*

The great craft shot across the Southern Colorado valley at a speed exceeding that of the fastest planes, then slowed and hovered over a dry patch of grazing land. In the control chamber, pilot-creatures beamed an ultra-violet scanner down toward the ground. As the ship passed over a small stream, the scanner picked up a signal. The pilots revised their approach angle to home in on the signal.

The signal was coming from an implanted electrode on the flanks of a cow.

The craft slowly descended.

In the cargo hold, a section of protective sheeting slid back from the viewing aperture. Mike could see the reddish hues of the rocks on

119

the ground as the craft approached it. Then he could see the cow.

The craft hovered over the grazing animal. The cow gazed up curiously. A beam of light shot down from the craft, enclosing the cow, then slowly lifting it into the air. To Mike's amazement, the cow was raised on the light-beam into the ship itself. There were metallic sounds in another part of the craft—hatches opening and closing? A few minutes went by. Then more noises, and the cow began to descend back toward the ground. But now it was only the stripped, gutted, whitish *shell* of the cow. It was transported on the beam of light back to the earth and laid delicately on its back, legs sticking up in the air. Then the ship began to move again. The covering of the cargo-hold window slid shut, and Mike could see no more.

The craft moved north at great speed.

In the cargo-hold, Mike stared helplessly at the three other human beings whose glass boxes were down the aisle from his. If only he could speak to them, and they to him, perhaps he could find out something more. Instead their eyes alone communicated—in mutual helpless terror and fear. No doubt the others were hoping *he* would help *them*.

The ship slowed over the Front Range and began to descend again.

*

George and his search party trooped through the snow, pausing warily every time a branch snapped or a bird called. After a forty-minute hike they were in the area where Mike had disappeared. They had found nothing—no tracks, no signs of anything moving on the ground. The new snow was pure and deep.

"Let's go on to the old tunnels," George suggested. There was reluctant agreement among the members of the search party; they plowed single file through the woods toward the canyon wall.

*

In his cabin Hiram Rowder was frying up some bacon when the

120

craft came over again. It shook the floor-beams. He glanced up, irate, and cursed the space people, shaking his fist at the ceiling.

"All this racket you're making will catch up with you some day, you sons of bitches," the wizened old miner yelled at the top of his lungs.

*

Mike guessed the ship was landing: the rumbling noise of its engines tapered off, then stopped. There was no way of finding out where they were; the viewing aperture was closed. Mike saw the same waves of apprehension he was feeling reflected in the eyes of the other captives.

There was silence for a while, then a door opened at the rear end of the hold, and four creatures entered. One of them was the tall spindly creature with the helmet; the other three were shorter, more human in appearance. The latter three wore skin-tight luminous suits that changed color, from grey to blue to silver, as they moved. The tall, spindly being wore a suit that looked metallic, shiny, and segmented. It occurred to Mike that this may not have been a suit at all, but the creature's *skin*. Again a chill ran down his spine.

The creatures passed among the cages, apparently making notes and communicating telepathically; they studied each captive, including Mike, and at intervals turned to each other and exchanged eye movements. Then they all left. A few moments later, the cargo hatch opened again and the humanoid with the pleasant voice entered. He came over to Mike's box and stared at Mike in a way that Mike couldn't help feeling was more "humane" than the scientific glances of the creatures who'd just left. "Or am I imagining things," Mike asked himself, "trying to assign a friendly nature to this character just so I can build up my hopes he'll help me escape?"

The creature's eyes moved in the way Mike interpreted as a smile.

"We would like to be your friend," the voice inside his head said. "But we cannot help you escape."

Mike was dumbfounded. He could keep no secrets from this creature.

"That is correct. We are aware of your thoughts—all of them."

121

"How do you do it?" The question leapt into Mike's mind almost involuntarily.

"It is a matter of awareness," said the voice inside his head.

"But I can hear *you*—"

"Only when we choose."

"So that's why I can't hear what those others—"

"Correct. You read us only when we choose."

"I see." Mike was ready to believe anything now. It was too late to consider credibility. Experience was teaching him to take everything on its own terms.

"Where are we now?"

"We are near your home. At our minerals recovery depot."

"Are we under the ground?"

"That is correct."

"But how can such a big ship—"

"It is a matter of what you call technology."

Mike's mind was temporarily silenced. He stared into the creature's large, pale eyes and wondered about Helen and the boys, and whether he'd ever see them again.

"It is difficult for you, but you must return with us to our base," the voice said in reply.

Mike's thoughts went blank.

"You will not experience pain," the voice said consolingly.

"What does *that* mean?" Mike had a creepy feeling that he knew already.

"You will be used in experiments," the voice said.

"Like those experiments you do on cows? Cutting their insides out?"

The voice was silent.

"And suppose I don't like the idea?"

"You have no choice, friend."

Mike felt like screaming. "Don't call me that."

"As you please. We wish to be your friend."

"You say 'we'—"

"This is our only first person form."

"Well, if you want to be my friend, get me out of here."

"That is impossible. You are in our charge. We must return you to our base for experiments. It is in our orders."

"Suppose you just let me go, would I be missed?"

"You would be missed. We would be deactivated."

"Deactivated? What's that?"

"If we function improperly we are deactivated upon our return to base."

"Deactivated is like—dead?"

"Correct."

"I see."

Mike's despair was the only thing left for the creature to "read."

The creature passed on to the other cages, and stopped and stood in front of each of them for a long while. Mike had an idea the creature was making his rounds like a kind of chaplain, trying to accustom all his captives to their fate.

*

Helen sat at the kitchen table listening to, or rather *feeling* the wind shake the house. Thank God for school, she thought. This is the worst it's ever been. I'm glad the boys don't have to hear it.

The whole house buzzed and hummed like some kind of telecommunications station gone berserk. The lights flickered on and off as brief power outages kept occurring.

Directly under Helen's feet, the creatures had their minerals recovery depot. Some six hundred feet down, in a huge subterranean chamber they had spent nearly a year carving out of solid rock. They used electricity generated by the wind to run their drills and probes. None of this Helen knew. She simply thought she was going insane. She sat at the kitchen table, her head in her hands, wondering where her husband was, weeping and shaking, wishing she could remember the prayers she had been taught as a child. Certainly nothing *else* was working.

*

Tommy and Eileen rose late that day; Eileen made a pot of tea

123

while Tommy went out in the snow to cut wood. When he came in they drank tea and smoked what was left of last night's joint. Tommy threw an armful of logs on the fire. Eileen sat down in front of it and began reading a story in a magazine she'd brought along from Denver. Tommy sat cross-legged on the other side of the room with his guitar, picking out the notes of a tune he was composing. The hours went by. Outside the wind was blowing the snow around in what looked like a ground blizzard. Neither Tommy nor Eileen felt much like going out. The previous night's experience had left them with the feeling that there was something unfriendly out there in the storm. You could either wait and see if it was going to come back, or you could go out and look for it.

It was warmer inside, at least.

*

Hiram Rowder, who'd been using the remains of an old bottle of cheap gin to help him wait out the storm, was asleep in his easy chair with his feet up on the top of his potbelly stove, when the two furry things came to his cabin to get him. What Hiram didn't know about the mines in that area, no one did. The creatures who commanded the furry things were interested in Hiram less as a physical specimen than as a source of information.

Hiram never heard the high pitched signals the furry things exchanged, or the growling noise that came from the black box one of them carried, nor did he see the beam of light from the box that bathed his ancient bewhiskered countenance as he sank through the bottom of his alcoholic dreams into a state of deep hypnosis.

He couldn't wake up or move. The two furry things had to carry him.

*

George led the way, Buck followed him, Spencer and Darrell brought up the rear some yards behind.

The two buddies were amused by George's cautious behavior as group leader.

124

"Some kind of point man, ain't he?" Darrell said. "Every time he sees a damn rabbit track you'd think he was about to step on a land mine."

Spencer laughed, remembering the hours he and Darrell had spent on jungle trails together, and all the dead lieutenants they'd cleaned up after.

Suddenly there was a yell up ahead of them, and then a shot. The snow made for slow going, and the trees were close together—they'd lost sight of George and Buck. Now they slogged through the snow, rifles ready.

Over a small rise they spotted George, who was down on his belly in the snow. Buck was lying in the snow on his back a few feet away. Mike's .32 was in his hand. There was steamy breath rising over George's head, but not over Buck's. Buck's eyes were open but he wasn't moving at all. The top half of his body was no longer connected to the bottom half. The two parts had been cleanly separated at the waist, where there was a space wide enough to see the snow through.

"Get down," George hissed, motioning to Darrell and Spencer, who were silhouetted against a grey sky at the top of the small incline. The two buddies dropped to the snow in a reflex action they'd learned years before in the Marine Corps.

Ahead of them they could see the canyon wall, and the shaft opening. In the underbrush at the mouth of the tunnel there was a black box that was growling at them and shooting out beams of light that seemed to be scanning the woods. The beams passed a few inches over Spencer's and Darrell's heads as they lay face down in the snow. Above them, twigs snapped and dropped to the snow, smoking.

"Shit!" Darrell whispered hoarsely, looking up.

"You said it," Spencer said softly.

"Must be some kinda goddam *laser*," Darrell said.

"Shut *up*," George hissed from his spot on the ground ahead of them. "Them sumbitches can *hear* us."

*

David Stanley, age ten, and his brother Charlie, age eight, got off the Basecamp Elementary School bus at the turnoff to the Stanley ranch and started up the ranch road, which was flanked by deep snow drifts.

It was the boys' first mountain winter, and their first big snow; naturally they were making the most of it. Instead of walking straight down the road to the ranch, they took a detour through the corral.

Mike had been doing some tree-thinning in the pine woods at the edge of the corral, and had stacked cut trunks and branches into a pile three or four feet high and ten or twelve feet long. The boys had turned this pile into a snow fort, which they took turns defending. It was Charlie's turn to hold the fort.

David went into the woods to wait while Charlie made snowballs. Then he packed a half dozen of his own, put one in each of the four pockets of his parka, and mounted his first assault on the fort. Charlie drove him back with a torrent of hard-packed snowballs. David ran off into the woods and circled around to the other side of the corral, where he would have the advantage of surprise.

As he high-stepped through the woods, a strong gust of wind came up and blew the snow around him into a blizzard-like swirl. David was only thirty or forty yards into the woods at this time, but the blowing snow cut off his visibility and he could no longer see out between the trees to the corral. The snow had also covered most of the familiar ground landmarks, and all David had to orient by were the trees—all of which looked the same. Intending to proceed in an arc that would bring him out at the north end of the corral, he made the arc too broad and in a few minutes found himself plunged deep into snow-blanketed forest terrain he didn't recognize. Instead of stopping to get his bearings, he kept on going, compounding his error. Soon he was lost and knew it. Blowing snow had already covered his tracks. He called out to his brother, but the wind was blowing hard, and it was just as difficult to hear as it was to see. David was getting tired and worried. There was no more than an hour of daylight left. After that, he knew, there would be something to get *really* scared about. He kept on walking, hoping he would simply happen on the right direction and find his way out of the woods by accident. With every step he got closer to the limits of his courage, which were no more extensive than those of any ten-year-old-boy. Then two things happened which put him over the limits. Ahead of him in the snow he saw a set of tracks which stopped him dead. The tracks were those of some large being whose foot had a tripod shape. Each track was the print of three large, rounded toes. The tracks were at least a yard apart. As David examined them, snow blew into the prints and began to obscure them. They had to be very fresh.

A moment later David heard a high-pitched moaning noise, like something mechanical. He froze, wanting to bold and run, but unable to do so. The seconds went by. Then he heard the noise again, closer this time, and ahead of him through the blowing snow he saw a bright light.

*

Spencer and Darrell huddled behind a rock at the crest of the small rise. George and the two halves of Buck were sprawled out in the snow ten yards ahead and below them. Beyond, in the underbrush at the foot of the canyon wall, the black box emanated sounds and lights that kept changing in timbre and hue but did not stop. The light beams seemed to be scanning the area, looking for something. They were playing over George's head now, coming closer and closer with each sweep.

"George," Darrell said as softly as he could. "Man, you better make a run for it."

George was already thinking the same thing. After one sweep of the beam had passed just six inches above his head, he sprang to his feet and dashed up the slope. The light followed him. He dove for cover behind Spencer's and Darrell's rock, belly-flopping into the snow. Realizing he was temporarily safe, the sheriff let out a sigh of relief.

"Well, boys, whatever that is out there, it sure don't mean us no good," he said. His voice came out in breathless gulps.

"What in hell happened to ol' Buck?" Spencer asked him.

"Damn fool," George blurted. "Took a shot at it."

"At what?" Darell's eyes were wide.

"Big hairy monkey we spotted down there by the old Happy Valley shaft. Winged him, too, I'm sure of it. The thing lets out a funny yelp like a hurt dog and jumps off into the brush. Then this box opens up on us, point-blank. It just sawed Buck in half. My God." George's face was dead white, his lips nearly blue with hypothermia. The shock of what he had just seen was adding to the effect of exposure to the elements. Both Spencer and Darrell knew immediately that they'd have to get him back to the ranch quick to keep him from freezing to death.

While they were considering their options, the menacing hum of the box abruptly ceased. They looked out over the top of the rise, and could no longer see the beam of light. They *did* see a large, dark, hairy shadow step out from behind a tree, and move off along the canyon wall, with the box tucked under its arm. As it moved it made a piercing, whistling cry that definitely resembled the forlorn howl of a beast in pain.

Spencer and Darrell wasted no time. They pulled George to his feet and helped him back down the slope into the woods, in the direction of the ranch.

*

The furry thing had been wounded, but it did not bleed. As it moved through the woods, small clumps of a fleecy white substance oozed from the spot on its flank where Buck's bullet had penetrated. The white fleece blew off in the wind, mixing with the flying snow and becoming indistinguishable from it. Limping slightly, the furry thing clambered through the scrub woods at the edge of the canyon wall, heading for the mine shaft entry, letting out small cries of pain as it went.

Then it sensed an intelligent being in the area, blocking its path. It stopped, extended its infra-red sensors, and perceived David Stanley. It could "see" David coming through the trees, some twenty-five yards ahead. The boy was on a path that would lead him directly to the mine shaft opening.

The furry thing had no orders concerning beings of David's particular size. It waited, extending its sensing field, which now told

128

him the young human was waiting too. They had noticed each other.

*

The search party had arrived safely back at the ranch, but were having difficulty getting help.

The power was out, and the telephone wasn't working, so George couldn't call Basecamp for reinforcements. The radio in his sheriff's department car was dead also, he discovered. He decided to drive into town, but couldn't get the car into gear.

"Transmission's shot," he told Spencer and Darrell. "Hell of a time for *this* to happen, ain't it?"

"You stay put, George," Spencer told him. "You don't look too good no-how. Me and Darrell will drive in, you hear?"

George agreed, but when they got in their water department truck the boys found that it was suffering from a transmission problem similar to the one in George's vehicle. They couldn't get the pickup into gear.

"Can't understand it," Darrell said. "Just changed the transmission fluid the week before Thanksgiving."

Spencer shook his head. The events of the day had surpassed his understanding.

They tried Helen's car, and then Mike's. Both were suffering from transmission problems.

"Them goddam space people are pushin' their luck, if you ask me," Darrell said in exasperation, blowing on his fingers after two hours of tinkering under hoods in the chill wind and drifting snow. "Goin' around wrecking people's cars! Somebody's goin' to pay for it!"

The men went inside and drank hot coffee with rum. Helen had produced the key to Mike's liquor cabinet, and told her guests they were welcome to the contents. Distraught, she herself drank cup after cup of black coffee, afraid to sleep in case Mike should return. Besides, the whole house was humming and groaning too loudly to make sleep possible. She put more logs on the fire and sat in front of it, thinking, while George and Darrell and Spencer sat in the kitchen and drank.

129

It was four-thirty before Helen noticed that the boys were unusually late in getting back from school. She put on a coat and went out to the corral to call them. She found Charlie alone in the snow-fort, crying.

"Darn old David played a trick on me again," Charlie sobbed to his mother. "He was s'posed to come back and attack the fort, but instead he's hiding out there in the woods, tryin' to get me scared. Why does he do that, Mom?"

Helen called at the edge of the woods but David did not come. She ran back to the house with Charlie at her side, and told the men what had happened. Spencer and Darrell went out to look for David. Half an hour later they came back without him. It was getting dark.

*

Hiram Rowder could appreciate the good treatment he was getting from the creatures on the ship. He couldn't move, of course, inside the glass box they put him in. Other than that, he was having a fine time, flattered by the space creatures' attentions. All the questions they kept popping into his head about the old mines gave him the definite impression he knew more about what things were all about down deep under the earth than even they did. Maybe they knew more about the sky, but subterranean stuff was Hiram's province. He enjoyed the position of respect the space folks were obviously ready to accord him. No doubt once they got back to their planet they'd let him out of this dang box and give him a nice home, or maybe even his own space ship. Inside his glass box, Hiram's old eyes shone in anticipation.

*

Joe Beauregard couldn't understand it. The weather was bad, sure, but for the first time in years he opened and closed the Frontier without drawing so much as a single client for the whole evening. Joe had heard stories of business being bad during storms in the Front Range, but never anything like this. The worst of it was the lack of conversation. To Joe's way of thinking, a man who had nobody to talk to was as good as dead.

It must be them damn space people again, he told himself bitterly, vowing to get even with them for ruining his business and robbing him of his good company. A man had problems enough to deal with in this life without competition from other worlds, he felt. That was just too much. He contemplated writing a letter to his congressman about it in the morning.

At a quarter to twelve he closed the bar down and went home to bed.

*

Tommy and Eileen spent the afternoon quietly in Tommy's cabin, reading and listening to the wind, and talking. After dinner Tommy suggested going down to the Frontier for a drink. Eileen said she'd rather they spent the evening alone together.

"We can have our own party," she told Tommy mysteriously, then went into the bedroom and rummaged around in her bag until she found a bottle of Bristol Cream Sherry she'd brought along for just such an emergency.

"Surprise," she said, coming back into the main room of the cabin with the bottle and a big smile. Tommy jumped up and kissed her.

"We can dance too," he said.

Tommy had no tape or record player, partly because he couldn't afford them and partly because he believed a cabin in the mountains ought to be as free as possible of the "60 cycle hum" which electrical systems create. He had electrical outlets in only one room of his cabin, the kitchen. The living room and bedroom were lit with candles and heated by wood fires. Tommy liked the feeling he could close the door to the kitchen and restore the rest of the cabin to its original condition, the state it had been in during its occupancy by the hard rock miners of the Happy Valley.

Tommy felt that as much as the miners' ghosts probably disliked the AC cycle, they also enjoyed music, so he kept a portable radio. It was in fact a practical necessity, since life in Basecamp in the wintertime was largely weather-dependent, and everybody in town needed a radio that could pick up the National Weather Service forecasting

131

station, located at 167 megaHertz on a VHF hi tuner. Tommy owned a "Patrolman CB-6," which picked up not only AM and FM, but VHF, UHF and CB channels.

He now turned on a Denver rock and roll station. Eileen helped him roll back the rug in front of the fire, and they opened the sherry, drank a glass each, smoked what was left of Tommy's minute stash of grass, and began dancing. In twenty minutes they had completely forgotten the weird vibrations which had been casting a pall of apprehension over the past few days.

The radio was playing a Grateful Dead song Eileen loved. She danced with her eyes closed, her arms stretched high above her head, exactly as she'd done at Red Rocks on the summer night Tommy had first met her.

Smack in the middle of the song the radio went dead. Eileen stopped dancing.

"Damn me," Tommy said, banging his forehead with his fist. "I knew I forgot to do something in town yesterday. Buy batteries."

Ellen sat down, disappointed. "That's all right," she said.

Tommy fiddled with the fine tuning to see if he couldn't coax a final spasm of power out of the radio. It was no use. Frustrated, he reached to turn it off. Just then a voice came over the radio.

"Attention," it said. "Do not be afraid. Repeat. Do not be afraid."

Tommy and Eileen exchanged stupefied glances. Tommy's hand fell away from the dial.

"Your appliance is interfering with our circuits," the voice said. "Cease operation of it immediately. Repeat. Cease operation of it immediately."

There was a long silence, then the entire message was repeated again. And again.

Tommy suddenly had an idea. What if it was some kind of practical joke—a CB broadcaster, say? He began switching the selector dial from band to band. He found the same message on various wave lengths and on AM, FM, CB, VHF hi and lo, and UHF. Each time the broadcast came in on a new band or wave length, he and Eileen felt cold chills. The short hairs were standing up on the back of Tommy's neck, under his pony tail.

"Well," Eileen blurted abruptly, "why *don't* we turn it off, if that's what they want?"

Tommy switched the volume dial to "off." The voice stopped, mercifully. Tommy and Eileen held on to each other tight, listening to the wind blow and trying desperately to pick out signals or signs in the miscellaneous noises of the gusty night.

*

David knew the thing that had made the funny tripod tracks, the thing that was flashing and beeping, would surely get him if he didn't think fast. He tried to imagine what his father would do in this situation, what any hero would do. His mind raced. He looked around wildly. To his right the canyon wall was largely concealed by snow-quilted underbrush. In the failing light David glimpsed a black opening there. It was the mine shaft. He shuddered. Still, if he could get there before the thing caught up with him, perhaps he could hide, maybe it wouldn't see him. . . . He ran through the snow, pushed the snowy branches aside, dashed headlong into the black hole in the mountainside. There were noises of branches breaking behind him. He tripped over the old rails and the icy litter of rocks at the shaft opening, sprawled on his face, jumped up and in panic too great to admit the fear of such a place, ran forward into the dark dark tunnel.

*

David's father was less than a mile away, still motionless inside his glass box. The cargo hold had a new inhabitant. Two human-looking creatures had entered sometime earlier—Mike had lost the ability of determining lengths of time, it might have been minutes or hours— and had put Hiram Rowder into a glass box. They had examined— or interrogated?—him briefly, then left. Hiram's eyes were glazed when they first brought him in, making Mike suspect he was drunk, and during the examination they turned even blanker; evidently the old man was asleep. Or perhaps he was just faking. The old boy was cunning, that much Mike knew. Either way, Mike couldn't make eye-contact with him, and as far as he could tell Hiram didn't even know he was there.

133

Mike's eyes turned back to the other caged humans. The boy appeared to be sleeping with his eyes open. The two young women were staring pleadingly at Mike, as they'd been doing for hours. What could he do to save them, when he couldn't save himself? Mike sent back glances of helplessness and despair, but the girls went on pleading with him. He looked past them at the dark wall of the cargo hold, trying to make his mind a blank like Hiram's. In a while he had succeeded and was asleep himself.

*

The sound of David's own footsteps in the tunnel terrified him, but what frightened him even more was the thought of what might happen if the unknown thing caught him. So he kept on, and kept on. But then he ran into a point where the ceiling of the tunnel had caved in, and he had to stop. He sat down on the cold rocks, panting, hearing his heart pounding in his chest. The tunnel was silent. Then it wasn't.

Far back down the way he had come, he heard a high-pitched beeping noise that was almost plaintive. It came closer and closer.

*

George had delayed telling Helen about what had happened to Buck. He meant to do so, but then when David turned up missing too, he knew he wouldn't be able to. Helen seemed to be in shock, and she didn't inquire about Buck at all. Either she had forgotten about him, in her distraction, or she sensed something about what had happened to him, and was afraid to ask. Helen was a very sensitive woman, George knew. He hadn't known her long but he could tell. She certainly wasn't much like his own wife, in that respect.

After Spencer and Darrell set out on foot from the ranch toward Basecamp to get assistance, George sat in the Stanley's kitchen and helped himself to Mike's liquor. The bottle of Bacardi had disappeared rapidly into the coffee cups of the three search party returnees. Now George was halfway through a fifth of Jack Daniels and had no intention of stopping while he was still conscious. He had given up on trying to pour his drinks into a shot glass which refused to stay put, and was now swigging directly out of the bottle.

In the next room Helen sat on the sofa in front of the fireplace, staring abstractedly into the crackling flames.

She knew damn well what had happened to Buck Warburton. She'd overheard Spencer and Darrell talking in the kitchen shortly after their return from the search. Helen and Mike had known Buck for nearly ten years. They were old and close friends. Helen had even met Buck's mother, a nice old lady who lived in Grand Junction. Now Buck was lying out there in the snow in pieces. If that had happened to her friend, what was happening to her husband and to her older son?

Outside the wind was howling. The house was creaking and humming as it always did in a windstorm. The candles in the living room kept blowing out. Helen was too involved in her thoughts to relight them. She sat in the dark room before the firelight.

Charlie was sleeping upstairs, fitfully. Helen heard him cry out in his sleep twice. She did not go upstairs. The day had been too much for her. She had not slept for two nights. Now another morning was coming. Helen didn't know if she could take what another day might hold. All her thoughts were in a tangle. If only she could let go of the tangled ball, it might somehow miraculously unravel. She closed her eyes. She dozed.

In the kitchen, George had passed out, his head, chest and arms sprawled on the kitchen table in an attitude of total repose.

There was a sound outside the house which no one heard except Charlie, who had fretted himself awake upstairs. Then there was a sound in the kitchen. The door liquefied, coalesced, fluttered like a thin membrane, but George did not see it happen. Through the melting substance of the door walked a tall, spindly, segmented creature with a transparent helmet and very large eyes. The creature walked slowly past the oblivious sheriff at the table, stopping to peer at him intently for a few seconds, then passed on into the living room. He bent over Helen's sleeping form, staring at her for several minutes. Then Charlie cried out upstairs.

"Mom!" The boy's voice echoed through the house.

Helen opened her eyes, and looked into the enormous eyes of the helmeted creature. She felt at once wide awake and totally paralyzed. It was as if the creature were draining out the contents of her brain through the eyes. Helen's head hurt. She wanted to close her eyes, to scream, to strike out at the creature, but she could do none of those things.

The creature continued to examine her. Helen began hearing questions in her head. She did not want to answer, but her mind answered for her.

Then Charlie cried out again. Helen broke from her trance. She shook her head violently, trying to clear it. The tall spindly creature was no longer there. Helen struggled to her feet, ran upstairs to comfort her son. As she went past the kitchen door she saw the sheriff's thoughtless head lolling from side to side on the table. George must have been dreaming. He was snoring loudly and talking in his sleep, something about "the ground. . . the ground."

*

David was a light weight in the furry thing's arms. He was cradled under one hairy arm, the black box was tucked under the other. David was too relieved to be scared. The thing didn't want to eat him. It only wanted to take him somewhere. Probably to meet his Dad. That was fine with David. It was what he wanted, what any hero would.

Somehow the furry thing found a way through or over the rock slide in the tunnel—David wasn't quite sure how, but soon they were past it, and the furry thing was loping along at a pace three or four times as fast as David himself had been able to manage. It seemed the furry thing could see in the dark, for it negotiated even the sharp corners gracefully and with barely any break in pace.

Soon they'd come to a part of the tunnel that was lit at the other end. David looked ahead and gasped. The light was bluish, greenish, orange, gold, all at once. Then as they grew closer the light got pure white, and very very bright. David could no longer look. He hid his face in the creature's fur, which smelled rank and wet.

Suddenly they had emerged from the tunnel and were in a large brilliantly lit hall. The furry thing put David down on the rocky floor, at the feet of two tall, spindly creatures who were its superiors, and loped away down a corridor, listing somewhat toward the side of its body on which it had been shot by Buck Warburton.

One of the two human-looking creatures motioned to David to rise.

David did.

Then the boy began hearing voices inside his head. The talking went on for a long time. Toward the end he began to feel very sleepy.

*

The great craft, depleted of fuel, loaded with mineral and biological samples, rested in the subterranean hangar with its engines throbbing gently in pre-takeoff mode.

The creature with the pleasant voice was standing in front of Mike's glass box. Mike again had the impression there was something sympathetic in the creature's eyes. Maybe there's something to hope for, Mike thought. Maybe there's time.

The creature's voice was apologetic inside Mike's head.

"It is not pleasant to say so but your time on this planet is very short," the voice said.

Mike's mind filled with the question: How long?

"The time before takeoff is sixteen hours by your scale of reckoning," the creature told him.

"And then what?"

"A craft will arrive to relieve us, continue our sampling procedures."

"And what about us?"

"We will return to our base."

"For good?"

"After refueling and debriefing, we will receive new orders."

"And me?"

"This is not our decision. It is not pleasant to say so."

"I see." Mike's mind filled up with angry images. "They have no feelings at all," he told himself.

"We seek your understanding of our purpose," the creature said, overhearing Mike's thought.

"Your purpose? You mean what you're up to? I've got no idea."

"We seek to achieve our own survival."

"Fine, but at our expense?"

"We seek to co-exist with you, while sharing your organic and inorganic resources. Yours is a rich planet. Colonization is among our long term goals."

"Exploit, then colonize?"

"Correct."

"That sounds familiar."

"Oh?"

"The history of our planet is full of your kind of co-existence."

The creature's eyes rotated in frustration. It wished to make its point clear to Mike, but was having difficulty in doing so. Perhaps its superiors were correct in indicating that personal communication with the inhabitants of this planet was a waste of time. The creature had contacted and detained Mike as part of a standard operation. It was not a significant procedure, just a part of the routine. Yet something compelled the creature to show Mike the kind of consideration one shows an intelligent being. Perhaps it was inexperience. Mike represented the creature's first "capture." The creature's superiors, some of whom had made dozens of captures, were far less considerate to their human captives. By the standards of their highly evolved social technology, the human was simply a very low order of being. What small knowledge any human captive was found to have was duly extracted and filed. Certain humans with specialized knowledge were abducted for purposes of interrogation. Others, like Mike, were abducted as breeders for biological sampling. In either case, the behavioral guidelines indicated that humans should be treated in the same way as test animals and other experimental subjects. Still, the pleasant-voiced creature felt compelled to explain things to the human being in the box. The being had been deprived of future relations with the rest of its breeding chain, and the pleasant-voiced creature was responsible. The creature sensed something like regret in this regard.

138

"Your planet has resources intelligent beings in other parts of the universe have good reason to envy," the creature told Mike gently. "Sooner or later you will be forced to give these up. It is to your advantage to share them with us now. We are able to co-exist with you and also to prevent invasions of your planet by beings less considerate than we."

"Is that the party line?" asked Mike.

"Party line?"

"I mean are you telling me what *you* think, or reciting somebody else's policy?"

"Our goals are unanimous," the creature said inside Mike's mind.

Mike gave up, discouraged. He made his mind go blank and tried to imagine himself off fishing on a mountain stream with his sons— an image he preferred to his present surroundings. For a few seconds he succeeded in blocking the creature's words out of his mind. Then inevitably they began drifting back in, calm and reasonable. The creature was still talking about sharing the benefits of the Earth. Mike interrupted.

"What about your own planet?"

The creature hesitated, looked around, went on.

"Our planet's natural mineral supplies were misused at an earlier period in our history, and as a result are now nearly exhausted. During the period of mineral misuse, industrial by-products saturated our atmosphere, which now blocks off much of the light and heat of our sun. In consequence, we suffer from a congenital deficiency of vitamin D and from mass epidemics of a disease similar to what you call ricketts. These conditions are contributing to a general diminution of our stature and vitality over the course of the breeding cycle and are threatening our survival. It is our present imperative to find mineral and nutritional resources that will assist our survival. It is for this reason we have explored other planets, and other regions of your planet.

"The rivers which irrigate the great agricultural regions of your continent derive ninety-five percent of their water from the winter precipitation at their source in these mountains which you call the Rockies. Thus it is here that we focus our study of the nutrients from which your abundant food sources originally derive. Additionally it is here that the great compressional events of an earlier stage in your planet's geological history have formed rich deposits of many minerals necessary to our civilization as well as yours. We wish to obtain a share of these minerals.

"These two motives guide us to establish our major bases of operation in this part of your planet. And there is a third. It is here that much of your military technology is located. At a much earlier period of our history we have experienced the threat of misuse of nuclear elements. We know this threat well. We have installed monitoring systems in this region which allow us to maintain a close surveillance of your military activity.

"It is these factors which have influenced our decision to base our operations in your area, among others. By random selection you were elected as an experimental subject from this area. You have been examined, and fulfill all our biological requirements. We seek your understanding of the necessities which compel our behavior in your regard."

"That's nice of you," Mike replied.

"Your planet interests us for other reasons, too," the creature said. "On a behavioral level, your tolerance of error is most unusual. You allow error at all behavior levels without punitive genetic effects."

"How's that?"

"To put it another way, on our planet one who acts incorrectly terminates his breeding cycle and in many cases his own activity. This error is rejected from the genetic process by reverse selection."

"On your planet, one mistake and it's curtains?"

"Curtains?"

"Just an expression."

"One we haven't heard," said the voice in Mike's mind. Did the creature's eyes look sad?

"What is 'sad'?" the creature asked, reading Mike's mind.

"Never mind," Mike thought. "You wouldn't understand."

A membrane flickered down over the creature's eyes, flickered back up. Mike felt the pleasant voice begin to enter his mind again, then withdraw abruptly.

The cargo hatch had opened and two of the tall, spindly creatures had come in. The human-looking creature with the pleasant voice

stepped back, away from Mike's glass box. The two spindly creatures stared first at Mike, then at the creature with the pleasant voice,
who quickly turned and walked down the row of boxes, pretending
(Mike guessed) to be checking each one intently. The two spindly
creatures waited until the checking was over, and then withdrew
with the pleasant-voiced creature at their side.

Something made Mike feel the creature who had tried to be his
"friend" was in danger of getting in trouble for it.

*

"Where did you put my Dad?" David demanded. He looked all
around. The light was too bright. He had to shield his eyes with his
hand.

The tall, spindly creatures looked down at him.

"He is safe," a cold, metallic voice said inside David's head.

"Then why won't you let me see him?"

The two spindly creatures paused and communicated briefly on a
wave length David's mind was not capable of receiving.

David waited. He turned around. The dazzling light was less
bright in the area behind him. There was a long wall of opaque rock,
with panels of instruments arranged along it—screens and grids lit
from below, bluish-green and eerie-looking, and many dials and
levers and buttons. . . .

He turned back toward the dazzling light. The light was coming
off a big ship that was parked in front of him. As much as it hurt to
look, David made himself do so. What if his Dad was on board?
Between David and the ship the two tall spindly creatures were still
standing over him. They were looking alternately at each other and
at David, their huge eyes expanding and contracting. David felt
high-pitched signals passing in the air, just out of range of his hearing. The noise was like static. It hurt his skin, made his head feel hot.
He backed away a step. The spindly creatures did not react. David
looked over his shoulder. Lights on the instrument panels were
flickering on and off.

David turned and ran toward the wall of instruments. It was only a
few yards away. The tall spindly creatures turned in time to see him

141

approach the dim-lit panels. Their eyes dilated rapidly, the crackling of static electrically filled the air. David felt the back of his jacket smoking. He was only a step or two from the panels now. He felt very sleepy, too sleepy to go on. He fought the feeling of sleepiness and stumbled forward, his small body banging frontally into the wall of instruments. As he hit, his hands reached out reflexively for something to hold on to. Then he felt himself losing consciousness, collapsing. His hands and arms slipped down along the wall, sliding over buttons and dials and levers. The boy crumpled slowly to the cold floor. Everywhere on the wall of instruments new flashing lights and displays appeared.

David had created an emergency. It is something heroes sometimes have to do.

*

Mike heard the cargo hatch slide open. He looked. No one came through it. Then he heard something else—a roar. Not in his head—somewhere in the hold. He glanced around. Doing so, he felt not only his eyes move, but his neck also. He looked down. His feet were moving too. He waved one arm out ahead of him—it encountered nothing. His lungs burned, he felt choked. He took a step forward, another, and felt himself pass through a cold patch of air, the edge of an energy field of some kind. He sucked in air, three or four deep gulps of it. He was standing in the corridor between the rows of glass boxes. He looked back. His own box was empty. Up and down the row, the beings in the other boxes were stirring and moving.

The mountain lion had broken out first. It was prowling the far end of the aisle, roaring up at the ceiling of the dimly lit cargo hold.

Cattle were lowing, moving around in their boxes. An elk galloped by, fleeing toward one wall of the hold. The two young women and the boy were struggling against invisible bonds, grasping at nothing, and then they too were free, breaking out of their boxes into the corridors. Even Hiram Rowder was out and moving around. Hiram had spotted Mike and was hobbling his way when the mountain lion turned on him. The lion sprang and knocked Hiram down. There was a lot of noise now, growling and lowing and screaming.

Mike sprinted toward the open hatch at the end of the hold.

*

Power was out all over Basecamp. Nobody's car would start. Telephones weren't working.

Darrell and Spencer went to the Frontier first, then to Joe Beauregard's home. Joe wasn't happy to be awakened at two in the morning. He was less happy still when he heard Darrell and Spencer's news, and then shortly discovered that his own electricity, phone and car were on the blink. Joe got a flashlight and dressed angrily, then stumbled out into the cold after Spencer and Darrell. The three went to the home of George's deputy. The deputy sheriff responded only after five minutes of pounding at his door. He came into the snow cursing a blue streak about how his police radio was screwed up, he couldn't get calls in or out and what a time for it. Trouble out at the Stanley place!

The men split up and combed the town to rouse as many able-bodied individuals as they could. In half an hour they had a party of thirty assembled in the town square on Main Street. Shivering, swearing, attempting feeble jokes, the men clutched their weapons and wondered out loud what the hell was going on. The showdown with the space people had finally come, Spencer and Darrell told them. Some of the men weren't too sure they wanted any part of it. There were murmurs of dissent, and several men strayed away from the crowd and slipped back toward their cabins.

Tommy Berglund stood in the street half-awake, shuddering from the cold, his hands thrust deep in his pockets, hoping Eileen would be all right back at the cabin. Tommy had no gun, and doubted there was much he could do. But Basecamp was his town, and if it was in danger he felt a responsibility to help however he could. Two people were missing out at the Stanley ranch, another was dead, according to Darrell and Spencer. That was as serious a situation as Tommy could imagine. He waited in the street, shivering, shifting from foot to foot, as Spencer and Darrell and Joe and the deputy took turns outlining to the other men what they thought should be done.

"I say we all go back out there now, on foot if we have to," Spencer proposed.

"Some of you men who are too old to walk that far can stay in town and keep an eye on things," Darrell said, glancing around at several elderly members of the crowd.

The deputy sheriff suggested that he himself ought to stay in town to make sure the women and kids were safe.

"That is a chickenshit proposition if I ever heard one," Joe Beauregard grumbled. "What is a lawman good for if he has to hide behind women's skirts at a time like this?"

"All right," the deputy said reluctantly. "So I come along. But I think it's crazy."

"Hey, you!" Darrell suddenly called out toward several men who were shrinking back into the shadows at the edge of the crowd. "I don't want to see nobody runnin' off now, y'hear? You boys stay and we can put up a good fight. If we start runnin' off and hidin', we ain't got a *chance!*"

Ignoring this advice, men continued to slip away. In a few minutes only a dozen or so remained, and there was much disagreement among these as to what to do. A poll was taken by Joe Beauregard. Seven of the twelve men voted to go out to the Stanley ranch and see what was going on. The other five were against it.

When Joe announced that "The go's have it," a few subdued cheers rang out into the sub-arctic night.

Bundled up against the weather and loaded to the teeth with as many rifles and bottles of whiskey as they could commandeer on a half hour's notice, the men of Basecamp set out on foot for the Stanley ranch at a quarter to four in the morning. Spencer and Darrell, at the head of the ragged column, each took a goodly belt out of the first bottle Joe opened, and then passed it back along the line. After two or three strong shots, every man in the marching troop was dedicated to all-out battle against the space people in defense of their community. They sang old military songs as they marched along.

The singing sounded kind of hollow at first to Tommy Berglund, who was as cold and as scared as he had ever been in his life. Tommy turned his collar up over his face to ward off the blowing snow. He wondered numbly what he was doing on a mission like this one. Every hundred yards or so somebody handed him a bottle. Gradually Tommy gathered courage. By the time the group was a mile out of Basecamp, he had joined in the belligerent songs, pitching in timidly at first but before long bellowing at the top of his lungs as he stomped down the road, just like the rest of the men.

Tommy had heard of whistling in the dark. This was hollering in the dark. It came to the same thing, he decided. He sang louder and louder.

*

Eileen pulled the covers up and tried to go back to sleep, but it was no use: she was worried about Tommy. She'd tried to convince him not to go out with Spencer and Darrell and Joe, but Tommy had kept insisting it would be all right. "Nobody's going to hurt an innocent pacifist like me," he'd laughed, pulling his boots on and stumbling out into the cold. Men were perfect fools!

It was almost daylight. A grey light was beginning to show in the window. Eileen pulled the covers all the way over her head and curled up deeper into the big bed.

*

Mike plunged through two bulkheads that should not have been open. All the doors, hatches and bulkheads in the ship and in the subterranean base were operated by "mind-locks"; they had been built to open only when a series of coded telepathic signals were applied. Mike did not know the signals. The doors were open because the complex electronic circuitry of the ship and of the base had been disrupted by David Stanley's attack on the instrument panel in the main control room. The creatures who had put the circuits together and built the underground base had never bothered to build precautionary mechanisms against such an event as David's attack. In their society mistakes had been virtually eliminated—both deliberate errors and accidental ones. The makers of the instrument panel had never considered acts of sabotage when they were drawing up their blueprints. Such things did not happen in their world, where disobedience and lawlessness were unknown.

On the other side of the cargo hold Mike found a glassed-in observation corridor that seemed to circle the ship. He ran along it for ten or fifteen yards before he came to another hatch that led outside the ship. There was a gangway that went down to the rock floor of the brightly lit subterranean chamber. Mike ran down it. Ahead of him he saw the control panels. Two spindly creatures were standing at the panels, their long segmented arms moving rapidly over the rows of instruments. At the spindly creatures' feet there was a small thing on its hands and knees. The small thing saw Mike and cried out, "Dad! Dad!"

The spindly creatures looked up from the panels, looked at Mike, looked at each other. Static electricity filled the air of the chamber; Mike felt his hair stand on end. Now both creatures were looking at him, hard. He looked away. They were trying to hypnotize him. He kept his head down, fought off the waves of drowsiness in which the spindly creatures' gaze had engulfed him, and kept on going. His legs felt heavy, but still he ran. The creatures' eyes were burning holes in his head. He could feel his scalp smoking. David was running toward him. He grabbed the boy up in his arms and half-fell into a dark open doorway at one end of the control panel. There was some kind of antechamber, with luminous suits hanging on hooks. Mike felt the chill air of the tunnel hit him. He stopped, grabbed one of the suits, stepped into it hurriedly. The cold air was clearing his head. He took David's hand and dove into the darkness of the long tunnel. To his surprise it was not dark at all. The suit he was wearing seemed to be giving off light—enough to allow him to find his way. In a few minutes he and his son were standing breathlessly in the open air of the surface.

It was a cold, iron grey dawn on earth, but Mike had never seen a more beautiful one.

*

The spindly creatures summoned the furry thing and directed it to

146

pursue the two who had escaped. The furry thing loped off down the tunnel, a black box tucked under its arm.

Then the spindly creatures summoned the creature with the pleasant voice. The air crackled as they communicated.

"We shall regard the large earthling's escape as your responsibility," one of the spindly creatures signaled.

"Incorrect," the pleasant-voiced creature indicated. "Repeat. Incorrect."

"He is in your charge. If he is detained and returned to us, no report will be made. This is our order. Detain and return him."

"Order received." The human-looking creature with the pleasant voice turned away abruptly and went out through the outer hatch into the tunnel.

*

Mike and David had only a five minute head start on the furry thing. They were moving through the snow as swiftly as they could go, but the furry thing was cutting down the distance between them with every loping stride.

David's tongue was hanging out; Mike stopped and they rested. In the quiet white woods there was nothing moving. Then there was. Fifty yards behind them a branch broke. They heard a faint humming noise. David knew what was coming. He jumped to his feet.

"Dad!" the boy cried. "It's after us, it's after us!" He grabbed his father's arm and began to drag him along. Mike looked back, saw nothing, but heard the humming getting closer. He began again to jog through the snow.

*

George woke with a start and looked out the window. Snow was falling again. The wind had dropped. It was getting light.

The sheriff moved his arm. An empty bottle fell over. He set it back upright. Then he noticed a smell of smoke. It was coming from the other room. George got up and went in there; embers from the fire had spilled out of the grate and were smoldering on the brick

147

pavement around the fireplace. He took a poker and nudged them back into the fire. Then it occurred to him that no one was around.

He went upstairs and looked in the bedrooms. In the boys' room he saw Charlie and Helen asleep on the small single bed, the boy nestled in his mother's arms. George went back downstairs as quietly as he could and put on some water for coffee. He had a taste in his mouth that made him wonder if rats had been nesting on his tongue overnight. George never wanted to see another drink.

He sat down at the kitchen table and stared morosely out the window, waiting for his water to boil, trying not to let his dreams of the previous hours seep back into his mind. Whatever they had been, he had not enjoyed them and was glad they were over. It was a new day. Maybe something good would happen for a change. God knows this town is *due* for some good news, the sheriff told himself. He began thinking vaguely about a sweepstakes ticket he had purchased a few weeks before. Now if only he could coax a smile out of Lady Luck, for once. . . .

*

Helen stirred in her sleep and pressed Charlie closer to her. She was deep in a frightening dream. Mike and David were running through snowy woods to her, but something was following them. She could see them coming, but behind them she could see something else. It was dark and hairy, and something in its body was sending out a beam of light that was very bright and very, very menacing. She wanted to call out to her husband and her son to hurry, but in the dream her mouth would not make the words. She tossed and turned, unable to wake up, realizing she was dreaming, but helpless nonetheless. . . .

*

George saw something bright move across the kitchen window. He put his coffee cup down, his hand trembling, and picked up his pistol, which he'd laid on the table next to him. Then he walked to the window and looked out. Through the falling flakes he saw a

148

fair-haired creature in a shimmering space suit running across the snowy corral. It dragged a small boy along behind it—the older Stanley boy, George decided. George raised the window. A blast of icy air hit him in the face. He stood his ground, held his gun up, drew a bead on the running spaceman. His trigger finger itched to be squeezed. Cold sweat ran down George's face despite the temperature. He had the runner in his sights. He was ready to fire.

No. What if he missed and hit the boy? His arm dropped, the gun hand fell to his side. Something was wrong. The boy wasn't just being dragged—he was *running along beside* the spaceman. This George couldn't understand. Soon they would be behind the barn, out of his line of fire. He had to make up his mind. Then he saw something else.

Out of the trees at the edge of the corral emerged a large hairy thing, loping along on two legs behind the boy and the character in the space suit, who had by now disappeared behind the barn. Under one long arm the hairy creature carried a black box that seemed to be shooting out a bright beam of light. It was the same creature the sheriff had seen the day before, the same box that had cut Buck Warburton in half.

George stepped back from the window and rubbed his fists into his eyes, wondering if he was really awake, then looked out the window again. The hairy thing was real, all right. It too disappeared behind the barn. George jumped to his feet, dropped his gun on the table and ran out the kitchen door into the woods.

If he had stayed, the sheriff would have seen a fourth being cross the corral and then move out of sight behind the Stanleys' barn, this one wearing a luminous suit identical to the first runner's.

*

Mike yanked the barn door open and pulled David inside behind him, then jammed the door shut and barred it. He and David scrambled up the ladder to the loft and crouched there, waiting. In a moment there was banging at the door, and a high-pitched beeping noise outside it. The door began to smoke. Mike hugged David close. Father and son watched the barn door with the absorption of life and death.

149

The door began to shimmer, to flutter; it became transparent, like fluttering cellophane. The hairy thing came through it, stopped and looked around. Then it looked up toward the loft. The box under its arm whined angrily. Its glowing was so bright Mike and David had to look away. Their involuntary flinching movements caught the furry thing's notice. It focused its infra-red sensors on them, raised the box, and tuned it to deliver a beam that would not maim, but stun.

At that moment the human-looking creature with the pleasant voice also stepped through the door and addressed the furry thing telepathically.

"Sheathe the beam," it said firmly inside the furry thing's head.

The furry thing obediently stroked the top of the box, stopping its vibratory whine. The bright beam faded, withdrew, as if sucked back into the box on an invisible reel.

"Return to the ship," signaled the creature with the pleasant voice.

The furry thing loped out of the barn.

The creature with the pleasant voice looked up toward the loft. In its eyes was the amiable kind of light Mike had noticed before.

"Our ship is leaving soon," the creature said inside Mike's head. "Farewell, friend."

The creature turned and walked out of the barn.

David looked up at his father. "Dad, what's happening? I feel all creepy. Did that thing just *say* something to you, or what?"

Mike felt limp. He stared into his son's eyes for a long moment. "I don't know, David," he said. "Let's go find your mother."

*

The men of Basecamp arrived at the Stanley ranch three-quarters of an hour later, stone drunk to the man, singing and dancing and shooting their rifles off into the air to celebrate the new day. When Mike told them he and his son were safe, they grumbled in disappointment over their lost chance for glory, or made a show of it, and then trooped off into the woods behind the house in search of Sheriff De Silva.

150

*

Eileen had just dropped off to sleep when the whole cabin began shaking. Instantly awake, she ripped the covers off and ran to the door, pulling it open and looked out. The sky had cleared; the sun was shining down on the snow out of a sparkling blueness. A great white craft was passing overhead, its under-surface reflecting snow-light with a brilliance like that of a million diamonds. Eileen blinked. In that time it passed out of her vision. Now the mountains were all she could see to the west, where the great craft had disappeared into the darkness of last night's sky.

"Oh my God," she said to herself in silent awe. "How *beautiful*."

*

On the ship, Hiram's wounds were being treated by a spindly creature with a medical kit.

"You will recover soon," said a cold metallic voice inside Hiram's head. "Then we will communicate again and you will advise us about obtaining the minerals of your planet."

Hiram's eyes danced. "Oh I will, will I? I will *if the price is right*, you mean!"

The spindly creature did not appreciate the cackling laughter it heard in Hiram's mind. The spindly creature hoped the old earthling was not going to create problems. There were problems enough already. What with the escapes and the damage to the control panel and the defection of the human-looking creature with the pleasant voice, who had not returned to the ship, it had not been an altogether efficient tour of duty, the spindly creature was soon going to have to admit.

Printed August 1980 in Santa Barbara & Ann Arbor for the Black Sparrow Press by Mackintosh and Young & Edwards Brothers Inc. Design by Barbara Martin. This edition is published in paper wrappers; there are 500 cloth trade copies; 250 hardcover copies are numbered & signed by the author; & 26 lettered copies have been handbound in boards by Earle Gray, each with an original drawing by Tom Clark.

Photo: Robert Turney

Tom Clark was born in Chicago in 1941 and has banged around a fair amount since then. This, his twenty-fifth book—but only his first volume of short stories—appears at a time when Mr. Clark is unable to state his place of residence due to being in transit.